WEREWOLF OF MARINES
PATRIA LYCANUS

Book 2

Colonel Jonathan P. Brazee
USMCR (Ret)

Semper Fi Press

A Semper Fi Press Book

March 2015

ISBN-13:978-0692407486 (Semper Fi Press)

ISBN-10: 0692407480

Printed in the United States of America

This is a work of fiction. All of the characters, names, incidents, organizations, and dialogue in this novel are either the products of the author's imagination or are used fictitiously.

I would like to thank first my editor, John Baker. He has made me a better writer with his insights and keen eye for detail. I would like to thank my artist, Panicha Kasemsukkaphat for putting up with my demands on what I wanted for the cover. I think she delivered. Finally, I need to thank Ruben Rodriguez, William Nelson, Christopher Roberts, Bill Underhill, and TJ Curtis from the 03-US Marine Corps Infantry Facebook group for their assistance on military life in Afghanistan, to Mundiya. FDB, and Arsham in the Wordrefernce.com forum, and Marwat, Happy Khan, and Smarty from the Pashtunformums.com for their assistance with the Pashto language. All remaining typos and inaccuracies are solely my fault.

Original Cover Art by Panicha Kasemsukkaphat

Chapter 1

Corporal Aiden Kass scanned the area ahead, trying to pick out his best bolt path. To his right, the mountain rose almost straight up. To his left, the mountain fell away to a small river that had cut this nameless valley in the Hindu Kush. This was a prime kill zone should the Taliban decide to hit them.

Picking out areas in which to bolt if they got hit was an ongoing, automatic action, just as are breathing, putting one foot in front of the other and scanning for signs of the enemy. Walk, scan for Terry[1], and choose a route to get out of the kill zone and under cover.

Aiden hitched up the 140-pound pack, trying to get the straps in a more comfortable position. With his hidden strength, he thought humping the pack should be easier, but it still was a bitch climbing up and down the mountains at altitude, his ILBE[2] straps digging into his shoulders.

Aiden was assigned as an "operator" for Marine Special Operations Team (MSOT) 8229, call sign "Badger 29." He and Doc Redmond had been last minute additions to the team after two other team members had been injured in a freak accident at Hawthorne during final workups, but at least they were from the recon family. They had been yanked from battalion together and had not gone through the normal A & S, the Assessment and Selection, screening process due to the short timeline, but as both had Silver Stars, they were nominally accepted by the rest. Manny, their JTAC[3], had been a communicator before going to school and had come from there

---

[1] Terry: slang for Taliban, as in "Terry Taliban"

[2] ILBE: Improved Load Bearing Equipment, the Marine Corps version of the Army's MOLLE, the backpack and load-bearing harnesses that carry everything a Marine needs to live and fight.

[3] JTAC: Joint Terminal Attack Controller. This is a trained officer or enlisted man who can control close air support.

straight to the team. No one had actually snubbed him, but it was clear that he had to prove himself to the rest before he would be accepted.

The air was pleasantly cool at 5,000 feet, but Aiden was sweating as he labored up the rocky path. Since his transformation, he didn't tolerate heat as well as he used to. Born and raised in Las Vegas, he would have thought he would be used to the heat by now. At least the team was not out in the deserts at Helmand with most of the Marines in-country. They had met with the CG[4] and his staff there before coming out to FOB[5] Ballenstein along the border with Pakistan, and while Camp Leatherneck itself was a veritable oasis, a little slice of the US, the area around the base looked bleak and exposed and was brutally hot.

The Hindu Kush in which FOB Ballenstein was located, however, was beautiful, Aiden had to admit. The rugged mountains were not the empty peaks of the south. These were covered with a sparse evergreen forest that looked like the trees around Tahoe. Take away the fact that this was a major smuggling and Taliban route in and out of Pakistan, and Aiden thought it could be a nice tourist destination—that is if you ignored the utter poverty that settled over each small village like a blanket of despair. Aiden had only been to the US, Mexico a few times, Iraq, and Kuwait, so he didn't have much to compare Afghanistan with, but he couldn't imagine many places worse off. The people looked old and tired, even the young men and women. Most of the villages had no electricity or running water.

What might have struck him most, though, was the smell. Whether at Camp Leatherneck in Helmand or up here in the mountains, there was a pervading scent of ancient dust, death, and rot, or at least that was how it seemed to Aiden. And it wasn't just him with his heightened sense of smell. The others on the team all had mentioned it as well.

The trail they were climbing rose to about 6,000 feet before going back down the other side and into a small valley where the people of Marwat somehow scratched out a living. The 100 or so

---

[4] CG: Commanding General
[5] FOB: Forward Operating Base

people of the village probably lived just as their ancestors had, ancestors who had fought off invaders from Alexander to the Soviets—and now the Coalition forces.

As tail-end Charlie, Aiden had to keep swiveling his torso, the heavy pack resisting the change in momentum, to check their rear. If they were to get hit, though, he doubted that anyone would rush them from behind and below them. The muj[6] liked to have a terrain feature between them and the Coalition forces when they hit so they could fade away when it got too hot.

He turned forward again and tried to see if the point had reached the crest yet. Then it would be downhill for a klick, another klick through the ville, and four more to their objective. Six more kilometers of march. Six more kilometers of being nothing more than a pack mule.

The MSOTs had all the high-speed, low-drag equipment that the Marines or the other services could provide. The other four teams in the company, the "regular" teams, had the GMVs[7], the souped-up versions of the Hummers, to get around up north in their AO,[8] but for Badger 29, it was the trusty combat boot that got them to where they wanted to go. Their GMVs had yet to leave FOB Ballenstein—the terrain and paths just didn't allow for it.

Aiden let out a sigh as he saw the first members of the team reach the crest and disappear from view. He was still a good deal away and had some climbing to do, but with some of the team up and over, it was a mental relief.

A slight bit of movement across the valley and on the opposite mountainside caught his eye. Since his transformation, he seemed more attuned to movement, but objects that weren't moving were a little harder to discern. He stared at where he thought he saw the movement but couldn't see anything out of the ordinary—until the PKM opened upon them. Almost instinctively, he turned and ran back down the trail 15 meters to where a meter-high and two-meter-long rock jutted up along the trail and offered some protection from

---

[6] Muj: slang for mujahideen.
[7] GMV: Ground Mobility Vehicle. Modified Humvee's that give better performance and carry a greater variety of weapons.
[8] AO: Area of Operations

the other side of the gorge. He dove to the ground and was joined a few seconds later by Griff, the team's mechanic and the next man up from him in the march.

Within moments, the entire side of the mountain opposite him seemed to open up with flashes as rounds began to impact around them. An RPG went off, only to peter out and fall into the gorge below.

"Stupid fuckers," Griff said almost in disgust. "Didn't they make a range card?"

Aiden estimated that the muj were at least 650 to 700 meters away across the gorge. That was well within range of the PKM, which had a max effective range of 1,000 meters, but too far for the RPG, which could only fly 500 meters.

Aiden scooted over to the end of their rock cover and fired his M4 at the flashes across the gorge. The M4's 5.56 round could easily reach that far. Marines all qualified at 600 yards on the range, but with Terry hard to spot, Aiden was just putting rounds downrange, hoping to get a lucky shot in.

A moment later, the loud crack of a .50 cal round went off from the crest of the road. Javier had opened up with his Barrett[9]. Sgt Javier Herrera was the team's primary scout sniper, and with the big Barrett, 650 meters was almost point-blank range. Several of the Marines carried the SR-25[10], and while they could also easily reach out and touch the ambushers, they didn't have the emotional impact of the Barrett. In Iraq, at least, the hajji often broke and ran the minute the Barrett opened up. Aiden had heard that the muj were made of sterner stuff, but this was his first contact with them, so he didn't have any personal validation of that.

"Now we see if Manny's worth his shit," Griff said. At Camp Leatherneck, Griff and a few others who had been on the same team had said their previous JTAC was worthless, and everyone had been

---

[9] Barrett: The M82 or M207 Barret is a .50 cal recoil-operated, semi-automatic anti-materiel rifle developed by the American Barrett Firearms Manufacturing Company and used primarily by snipers.

[10] SR-25: a smaller sniper rifle based on the M16 family of weapons but firing a 7.62 round.

slow to accept Manny as part of the team. If he could call in air and break the ambush, then that would go a long way in acceptance for him.

An explosion sounded from about 30 meters up the trail quickly followed by another. Shouts sounded, more in surprise than anything else.

What do they have that can reach like that? Aiden wondered.

Another explosion sounded up the trail, but below them, and it quickly became clear. Someone was up on the mountain above them and throwing grenades over the edge and down at them. No one was hurt yet, but it was only a matter of time before a grenade landed on the trail itself and hit someone.

Aiden and Griff both looked up the side of the mountain. It wasn't exactly a sheer cliff, but it was unclimbable. From their route brief, Aiden knew that to get up there, someone would have to go over the crest and down into the valley ahead, then cut back and make the climb over an easier slope. That could take several hours, and this contact would be over by then.

"Motherfuck!" Griff said. "Those assholes over there pin us down while Terry up there drops grenades on our heads!"

"Air can take them out up there, right?" Aiden asked.

"Shit, think of it. An A-10[11] can use its guns, but if we get a Lancer[12], that's only bombs. And if he's only a few meters off, what happens?" Griff asked as he fired off another volley across the gorge.

Aiden had to think for a moment before realization hit him. "The 500 pounder comes down here and takes us out."

"If they use a 500 pounder. The Lancers also got them big 2,000 pounders. And even if they hit up there, that's a whole shitload of mountain breaking off and coming down the slope on our heads. We'll end up buried down there in the river," he said sourly.

Another PKM opened up, sweeping the trail. With the Marines prone, the mujahideen weapons were having a hard time

---

[11] A-10: the A-10 Thunderbolt II, known as the Warthog. A ground support plane that provides immense firepower against ground targets.
[12] Lancer: the B-1 bomber.

hitting anyone, but if they stood up, the Marines would present much easier targets for them.

Aiden looked back up the trail, where about 70 meters up, Javier was calmly putting out rounds. The big gun kicked, and the report echoed back and forth in the canyon, the reports of the other weapons being fired by both sides seemingly being made by pop guns in comparison. Suddenly, there was a flash of fire on the Barrett, and Javier fell back. Aiden's heart lurched, but Javier rolled back over and inspected his weapon. It was too far to see much, but the radio told the story. A PKM round had hit the gun, taking it out of action. Javier's hand was hit, but he was still functional. Without the Barrett, though, it was small arms and their SAWs[13] against the mujs both across from them and above.

A grenade landed on the trail and detonated, and a scream of pain reached the two Marines. One of the team had been hit. The Taliban had picked a perfect ambush site. The Marines could not move without exposing themselves to automatic fire. If they stayed until they could get air, the grenades being lobbed from above would slowly take them out. The situation was becoming dire, and something had to be done.

Aiden knew what that something was. He had thought about this over and over again before this deployment. If the situation arose where he needed to shift to protect his fellow Marines, he would do it, Council be damned. Hozan had warned him against shifting, especially after he had broken up the attack outside of Ramadi as a werewolf, but he couldn't just sit there and not do anything.

"I think I saw a way up the cliff back there a ways," he told Griff. "I'm going for it."

"What? I didn't see no path," Griff responded, popping up over their rock to fire a few more shots before dropping back down.

"It was not much, but I think it's a way up. I'm dumping my gear here, then I'll take a look again. If it isn't, I'll be back," he said.

"You'll get leveled as soon as you stand up."

---

[13] SAW: M249 Squad Automatic Weapon. A one-man machine gun firing the 5.56 round.

"Nah, they're putting most of the rounds up there in the middle. Besides, they'll just think I'm bugging out, and probably send someone to snatch me back there somewhere."

Griff looked unsure, but he asked, "Do you want me to go with you? Two're better than one."

With Griff there, he couldn't really shift, so he quickly said, "No, I need you to cover me. Let me look first, and I can always call you to come join me."

"Sounds like shit," Griff said, a round pinging off the top of the rock and sending rock dust over them. "But let me call it in first."

Aiden had already dumped his pack, and he said, "Get permission, and if Norm says no, tell him I've already gone."

He got to his knees, took a breath, and then jumped up and sprinted down the path. To his surprise, no rounds chased him. Maybe they did think he was bugging out. After only 100 meters, the path bent around the mountain, shielding him from the Taliban on the other side of the gorge. He looked up, and the mountain in front of him looked impossible. And to Aiden in human form, it probably was.

Quickly stripping off his battle rattle, frog,[14] and boots, he was down to his trou and body armor. With one more look up and down the path, he closed his eyes, and with barely an effort, he shifted. Within moments, his sense of smell and hearing sharpened, his color vision faded, and the intoxicating feeling of immense power poured through him like a pyroclastic flow. It had been months since he had made the shift, yet his varg body felt like an old friend embracing him.

The cliff wall in front of him, which had looked like an impossible barrier before, was now merely a challenge. With a growl emanating from deep in his throat, he jumped up, his powerful legs catching on rough spots and propelling him forward, the claws on his hands grabbing and pulling in his center of gravity. Rocks dislodged by his passing rained down. Several times, feet or hands slipped, but the forward momentum kept him going. Within

---

[14] Frog: the flame-retardant blouse worn by the military during the later stages of the fighting in Iraq and Afghanistan. The sleeves are digital cammies, and the torso is a one-color tan.

two minutes, he had climbed over 400 meters to the top of the mountain's shoulder. To his right another 100 meters away, the mountain continued to rise, but this was good enough. His prey would be on this wide ledge.

Aiden started a slow jog along the edge of the cliff, looking through the scattered trees to spot the Taliban fighters. He could hear the firing below, the sharp crack of the American 5.56 and the deeper report of the mujahideen's 7.62 rounds sounding much more distinct to his varg ears. Within moments, those ears picked up something else: Pashto.

Aiden's M4 was slung across his back, forgotten in the rush of being a varg again. He sped up, dodging the rocks and trees, his nose telling him that just ahead were four men. He could smell the adrenaline reeking from their pores. A few more steps, and he could see them, all dressed in the typical Pashtun dress. Three were busy pulling the pins and tossing grenades over the edge of the cliff while one stood guard, his AK at the ready. Only he wasn't looking behind them; he was watching his three companions toss the grenades. His bust.

Aiden never slowed down. He rushed the guard, who turned around just in time to see the apparition close in on him. He tried to swing his weapon around, but Aiden blocked it with one hand and took him by the throat with the other. The man gargled out something before Aiden swung him around and sent him flying into his companions who were only now beginning to realize something was wrong.

The guard hit one of the grenade throwers, knocking him over the edge and out of sight. Aiden took three long strides and was among them. One man had a live grenade in his hand. He threw it right in Aiden's chest, where it bounced back to fall just behind the man. The Taliban fighter realized his mistake, but between a creature out of his nightmares or a live grenade, he didn't know what to do. Aiden solved that problem for him. He picked up the man and threw him down, right on top of the live grenade. The man was stunned and weakly tried to move off of it.

Aiden turned to the other two. One took one look and started running. The other reached for a wicked-looking knife at his belt.

There was no fear in his eyes as he lunged for Aiden. In another time or place, Aiden might have admired the mujahideen. With his team in danger, however, there was no room for that. As the man lunged, Aiden hit him flush in the face. There was a crack—whether that was the man's jaw or neck, Aiden wasn't sure, but the man went down.

The runner who had fallen was crawling away, moaning in what might have been Pashto, but was probably mindless gibbering. Aiden looked back at the man on the grenade and wondered why it hadn't gone off. Was it a dud? He took a step closer when it did detonate, shredding the man and sending shrapnel into Aiden's legs, belly, and face. His flak jacket had protected part of his chest, but the rest of him sure felt the pain!

Of course, at 300 meters or so above the trail below, they would have had to adjust the fuzes on the grenades so they would not detonate too high above the Marines, hence the long delay before the grenade went off. Aiden wanted to slap his head in a "d'oh!" moment.

The sting of the shrapnel didn't put him in a very good mood, and he almost casually grabbed the runner by the legs and pulled him back. The man's mind seemed gone—it was time for his body to be gone as well.

Aiden carried him to the edge of the cliff where he was surprised to see the first man, the one who Aiden had thought had already been knocked over, clinging to some bushes on the slope. The cliff was not abrupt, as Aiden had expected. It went down at a steep angle some 30 meters before plummeting down at what had to be a steeper angle. The mujahideen had been throwing the grenades out maybe fifteen meters to clear the edge below.

Aiden hefted the man he was carrying. He probably weighed 200 pounds. Aiden was very strong in varg form, but that strong? There was only one way to find out.

He picked up the man and brought him to his shoulder. The varg shoulder joint didn't have as much motion as a human joint, but Aiden pushed off with his legs in a sort of shot put motion, sending the man flying. Aiden wasn't sure he would clear the edge, but most of him did, with only his feet catching on the edge, and that sent him tumbling as he fell down the cliff. Aiden wanted to roar with delight.

He picked up the guard, who was barely conscious, and he tried grabbing one leg and arm and by twirling him discus style this time, cleared the edge by a good meter or so. Discus was better than shot put, evidently, when throwing people.

Looking at the remaining two mujahideen, he decided to leave the one who had been killed by the grenade. He had fought, at least, without fear, and an unspoken warrior creed made Aiden leave his body alone.

That left the one on the slope below him. Aiden could let him live, but the man had seen him as a varg, and so leaving him alive was probably not a good idea. Aiden stepped over the edge and onto the first slope. He grabbed several bushes to keep his balance. It wouldn't do much good for him to fall over the ledge himself and hit the trail among his fellow Marines, even if his varg body survived the fall.

"Oh, hi guys. Don't mind me, I'm just your friendly neighborhood werewolf" wouldn't cut it.

As he approached the Taliban, the man simply said *"shaytan"* and spit on Aiden. He let go of the bush he was holding and started sliding down the slope on his stomach, eyes locked on Aiden's. It wasn't until he was almost at the edge of the cliff proper that he seemed to realize what he was doing, and his resolve faltered. Panic hit his eyes as he went over, and he screamed as he started his fall.

Rounds started zinging over his head. Evidently, the Taliban on the other side had seen their buddies fall and were firing at him. But it was a useless gesture. They couldn't even see him, and the edge of the cliff kept any rounds from impacting on the top. They must have just been enraged to see their friends bounce down the cliff and onto the trail, probably splattering into bloody red messes.

Oh shit!

A body falling from 300 meters could kill a Marine if it landed on him. His varg mind was caught in the blood lust, and he hadn't thought it through. He almost shifted back as the shock hit him, but he needed to stay in form to get back down.

There were four AK's and over 50 grenades up on the ledge. The AKs were easy. He took each one and, with a couple of hits against a rock, had put it out of action. The 50 grenades were something else. He didn't want to leave them there, and he couldn't take the time to pull the pins on each one and let them blow up. There was still firing going on below him, and he had to get back into the fight. He picked up the box and took it with him.

A few minutes later he was going down the mountainside. After less than 100 meters, when the slope got steeper, he ended up tossing the box ahead, knowing he could come back and police up the grenades. He hurried down, more of a controlled fall than a climb, although for the last 100 meters to the trail, he had to face the cliff and actually climb down. He hit the trail, looking back up for any sign of movement. The firing had fallen off some, but the firefight was not over yet.

Looking over the edge of the trail, he had another 200 meters down over jumbled rocks to the water, then what looked to be an easier climb back up the other side. Before he could think of a logical reason to take it easy, he bounded over the edge of the trail and bounced from rock to rock all the way to the bottom. Any parkour specialist would have been green with envy had they been there to witness his descent.

He splashed across the five meter wide tumbling mountain river and attacked the other side. He didn't know how many of his team had been taken out, but the longer it took, the more chances there were that a Marine could be hit.

It was easier on this side, and within a minute, he found a small trail leading up into the trees and rocks. It was barely more than a goat trail, but it led in the right direction. The firing got louder, and Aiden pushed his senses ahead. Through the heavy smell of gunpowder, he could pick up people, probably two in front of him. He slowed down, and could just make out the flash of white clothing ahead when another sound caught his attention. It was a high *rooooooshshsh* that confused him for a moment. It didn't confuse the two Taliban, however. Aiden saw a head pop up, looking at the sky. Immediately, the two men bolted, running only 10 meters beyond Aiden but never seeing him.

Like a dog seeing a rabbit run, Aiden almost instinctively took after them before his brain realized what was happening. Somewhere, up above him, at maybe 20,000 feet, a B-1 Lancer had just released its payload. This close to friendlies, it was probably the 500 pounders and not a 2,000 pound JDAM[15], but that was more than enough. Werewolves were amazingly tough creatures, but they couldn't stand up to the best the US Air Force had to offer.

Aiden wheeled and plunged back down the goat path, heedless of rocks or anything that might trip him up. The *rooooshshsh* got louder and louder, seemingly right on top of him. A sense of panic threatened to take over, and he had to push that down. From feeling invincible on the other side of the river, he had been reduced to a powerless mouse running for cover.

The first bomb hit behind him, the blast wave picking him up and throwing him 15 meters down the path where he bounced and skidded among the rocks. Then a heat wave washed over him, and his hearing was gone. Another blast sounded, somewhat fuzzy to his ears, but farther up the slope.

Face-first in the dirt and rocks, he pushed himself up and checked himself over. His ears were ringing, but he seemed to be in one piece. Just a few minutes later, and Aiden might have been right at the point of impact.

Lesson learned, he thought. *Get out of the way of the Air Force!*

The firing had stopped. The air strike had broken the ambush. Aiden guessed that Manny had just made the grade with the team.

He made his way to the river and up the other side to where he had stashed his gear. With a quick shift, he was back to human. His radio was buzzing for his attention. That was another thing he'd forgotten. They would have been trying to reach him for quite awhile and probably thought he was dead.

He pulled out the connector to his headset and shifted his right arm back to werewolf mode. He bent the connector prong so it couldn't fit, giving him an excuse, then shifted the arm back.

---

[15] JDAM: Joint Direct Attack Munitions, a guidance kit that uses GPS to convert unguided bombs into all-weather "smart" munitions.

Things had worked out this time, but he had gone off half-cocked, and it could have gotten him discovered at best, killed at worst. If he was going to use his abilities, he was going to have to think things through much, much better.

Chapter 2

Zakia sat in the afternoon sun, sipping her green tea. Most of her tribe drank *shomleh*, the salted, mint yogurt drink of generations of her people. But the British had introduced tea in her great-grandfather's time, and that was one habit that had caught on. No British *asker*[16] had been in her mountains since her father was a child, though. Zakia didn't know where they had gone. Now, the only *parangay*[17] were the other Pashtun in the village in the valley and the steady stream of Pashtun, Tajik, Haraza, and even Punjabi that used her mountains as a highway for travel and smuggling.

Like most Muslims, even if her tribe might be considered only nominally observant, she had a distaste for those who dealt in *teryaak*.[18] The smugglers, however, rarely left the trails, and so her people left them alone. The less attention drawn to her tribe, the better.

As if to emphasize the point, far off in the distance, somewhere down near the village, the sound of gunfire broke out. Zakia snorted, then took another sip of her tea. Yes, it was better to leave the world of men alone. The tribe needed very little from the outside world in their own small village, and that could be acquired from a handful of trusted Pashtun traders, men whose fathers and fathers before them had provided goods for them.

Like this lovely tea, she thought, ignoring the distant gunfire.

Two of the little ones ran across the dusty area in front of her house, screaming and laughing, lost in their games. They were the ones who had to be protected. They were the future of her tribe, a people who had been feared and hunted since the mountains rose up to the sky.

---

[16] *Asker*: soldier
[17] *Parangay:* foreigner
[18] *Teryaak*: opium

She drained the last of her tea but didn't get up. Time was not a pressing issue, and while a half-woven rug was on the loom in her home, she felt no compulsion to get back to it. It would get done when it got done, and that was good enough for her.

Qalandar, one of the oldest members of the tribe, came out of his home, spotted Zakia and hurried over to her. Most members of the tribe got along well with each other—divisiveness could be their downfall, and everyone knew that. Despite this, Qalandar tended to grate on her nerves. Stuck in the old ways—especially those of their human cousins—he had never been supportive of the tribe's leadership falling on her shoulders. He was not a problem, but sometimes an annoyance. She made an effort to smile as he walked up.

"Did you feel it?" he asked.

"Feel what, Qalandar?"

"Over there," he pointed over his shoulder down to the valley. "Someone shifted."

That caught Zakia's attention quickly. She didn't bother to question the old man. "Qalandar" meant someone not concerned with worldly affairs, a sort of mystic, and Zakia didn't know if he had simply grown into the name or if some other power had influenced his naming. Either way, Qalandar had the finest sense of their abilities and could tell when anyone shifted. If he said someone had made the transformation, then someone had.

For years, there were none of the Tribe in their mountains other than them. They knew that there were others. They knew about the Council that supposedly ruled over them. But that was out there, beyond the land they called home. They ignored this Council and stayed out of sight. It was bad enough that the humans hunted them, but to submit to this *parangay* Council was beyond imagination.

Could the Council of werewolves, who Zakia had thought had forgotten their small tribe, be on their trail?

"Gather the elders together, now," she told Qalandar.

The tribe had to be prepared.

Chapter 3

"And our spy? No one saw him?" COL Jack Tarniton asked?

"No, sir," MAJ Keenan Ward answered, glad that the colonel couldn't see his grimace at the word "spy."

The colonel was just too much into all of this, Keenan thought. "Spy" was a rather grandiose term for someone who was merely ordered to keep an eye on Cpl Kaas and report back any observations.

This entire operation was too cloak-and-dagger for Keenan, from getting Kaas into MARSOC, getting a secret MSOT formed and assigned to the regular MARSOC company being deployed, and then getting Kaas assigned to it. The "accident" that took two members out of the team still made Keenan feel guilty, even if he had had no direct part in that. At least the accident had been minor—it could have turned out worse for the two men who had been removed to make way for Kaas and HM2 Redmond.

Keenan would never have thought all this would be possible, but evidently, the colonel had more pull than a mere O6 should have. Not only did they form up the secret MSOT, but he got the team out of Marine control. While most of the Marines were in Helmand and the MARSOC company was supporting the Army's 101st Airborne Division along the Uzbekistan border, MSOT 8229 had been quietly attached to another Army unit, the 10th Mountain Division. If he could have, Keenan was sure the colonel would have transferred Kaas to the Army, but this was almost as good.

The fact that the area had long been rumored to be a haven for werewolves was not lost on Keenan, either. He was sure the colonel was well aware of that as well.

What had surprised Keenan was that the colonel had sent him, missing leg and all, to FOB Ballenstein as well, to keep an eye on their prize subject. He and MT had been assigned as a "special advisor" team to the company assigned to the FOB, where the company commander was sure the two were higher headquarter spies.

There's that word again: "spies," he thought as he listened in on the secured satphone.

"So Kaas climbs a cliff, throws off three Taliban and kills another, and no one saw him?" the colonel persisted.

"That's about right, sir."

"'That's about right, sir,'" the colonel mimicked, his voice raised high. "I will tell you what's 'right,' Major. What's right is that you are there for a mission, and you'd better accomplish it. You know damn well that he had to have changed into a werewolf. What he did was beyond any human's capabilities. But we need concrete, actual proof, and I'm expecting you to get it. Am I clear?"

"Yes, sir, 100 percent. I'll find out one way or the other," Keenan responded.

"You do that, Major. I've got plans forming here, but we need the proof," the colonel said. "Also, I don't like the fact that the friggin' Air Force is dropping heavy ordnance all around our boy with only an enlisted JTAC controlling them."

Keenan didn't understand the colonel's point. His tone of voice when he said "enlisted" left little doubt as to his opinions on the capabilities of enlisted men to control close air support, but the team needed the Air Force security blanket. If by some weird chance Kaas was more than he seemed, then it wouldn't do any good to get him killed by the Taliban.

"I want you to see about getting an officer JTAC with that team. And until then, I want you to approve any fire. The new CG's[19] ROE's[20] are trying to limit civilian casualties, so that is your excuse to canc any close air that could cause friendly fire accidents."

"Yes, sir," Keenan dutifully said but having no intention of following through on that.

The colonel didn't understand the Marines, and especially MARSOC. Sgt Manny Rugieri was not only competent, but he had graduated number one in his class, finishing ahead of officers in the class as well. The Marines would not take kindly to some Army

---

[19] CG: Commanding General
[20] ROE: Rules of Engagement

major telling them they had to get an officer JTAC on the team. No, that wasn't something he was going to tackle.

"OK, then. Let's get the proof I need. Give me a call tomorrow at the same time. Tarniton, out."

Keenan disconnected the phone and placed it on the small table next to his cot. Despite his mission, he still was not convinced that there was any such thing as a werewolf. Yes, Kaas had active blood cells that seemed to fight off infection. Yes, he was a badass fighting machine despite his deceptively normal appearance. But a werewolf?

He shook his head and lay back down, hoping to get a few more hours of sleep before morning. This was a dead end job. It was much harder to prove a negative than a positive. How do you prove someone is not a werewolf? But he knew "Tarnation" was like a rat terrier, and he wouldn't let go of Cpl Aiden Kaas simply because Keenan said the young Marine was just a normal human being.

Chapter 4

"Well, that's about all the time I have. It's been good talking to you," Aiden said as a soldier waited none-too-patiently for his turn.

FOB Ballenstein was way out in the sticks. The only electricity there was what the Army generators could produce. With no internet connection, communications with home were only over two satphones, and each person had to sign up for ten short minutes.

"OK, I understand. Miss you," Claire said from Camp Smith. "Keep your head down, OK?"

"Sure thing. You know me."

"Unfortunately, I do. Leave it to me to fall in love with a hero-type," she said.

Love? That still gave him a thrill when he heard it.

"Sorry, Corporal, you're time's up," the civilian contractor said, an overweight Filipino.

"OK, OK, I gotta hang up. I'll call again next week," he said hurriedly before cutting the connection and handing the phone to the attendant.

The man took the phone, logged in the waiting soldier, then handed the phone to him. Aiden had to wonder about the man. Who would take a job out in the mountains of Afghanistan with none of the trappings of civilization?

His call with Claire, though, had put him in a good mood. The "love" word had a way of doing that. He and Claire had an interesting relationship, to say the least. Claire was more gung-ho than he was, more dedicated to the Marines, and she took her career seriously. On the job, she was a no-nonsense Marine. As a very attractive and fit woman, she had her share of attention, but she didn't mix her professional life with pleasure and ignored every come on. When Aiden had met her, most of his fellow Marines assumed she was a lesbian because of that lack of interest in them.

In private, though, when out of uniform, she was totally different, and Aiden often got glimpses of the little girl that still made a home in her heart. He was proud of her professional achievements, but that little girl side of her touched him deeply. It had taken him awhile, but he finally realized that he loved her, and he was constantly amazed that she seemed to love him back. Girls just didn't fall for Aiden Kaas—at least not until he'd been infected. Sometimes, when he was in a pensive mood, he thought about his life, and he wondered if he would turn back the clock and keep out of that room in Fallujah, keeping away from Omar Muhmood, the patron he'd never really known. But if he hadn't become a werewolf, he knew Claire would never have gone out with him. For that reason alone, he knew he would have marched right into the room and been bit again, if given the choice.

Aiden had visited Claire in Hawaii after his last deployment and spent ten wonderful days there. The two had checked into the Hale Koa Hotel, the best hotel in which Aiden had ever stayed. It was right on Waikiki beach, next to a beautiful greenspace. The best part was that the room charge was based on rank—the lower the rank, the lower the rate. Claire was already a corporal, but Aiden was still a lance corporal waiting for his promotion, so they got the lowest rate available, about the same amount as a Motel 6 would be back in Vegas.

On about the third or fourth day, exhausted after lying on the beach, getting lunch, lying out by the pool with a mai tai, taking a nap on the pool chair, then getting up to shower and get dinner, they had gone online to check out the local clubs for a fun evening out. Somehow, they found themselves looking at real estate, and outside Camp Lejeune in Jacksonville, there were several neighborhoods, such as Northwoods, where a basic home could be bought for $60,000. That led them to the Navy Federal Credit Union site where they discovered that with the combined income of two corporals, they could qualify for a mortgage. That turned into a discussion of future duty stations.

They had never spoken about marriage. The thought was still scary to Aiden, who kept half-way expecting Claire to come to her senses and leave him. But with that evening, it seemed almost like a done deal. He wanted to make it official and ask her, but he chickened out, and when he left her to go back to Lejeune, nothing was planned. Now, sitting out in the Hindu Kush, he was kicking himself for not asking her. When he was with her next, if she seemed like she was expecting it, he would steel himself and ask. Really.

Aiden's stomach growled, and he checked his watch. He needed to get some food inside of him. With only one hot meal a day, mornings were MREs.[21] After the attack the day before, they had been recalled back to the FOB, much to their surprise, but they had missed hot chow, and Aiden had been starving. MREs were supposed to have all the caloric and nutritional needs of a fighting man, but they just didn't cut it with him. Aiden needed calories, raw calories. Shifting took a lot of energy, energy that had to be replenished.

He entered the tent that served as a DFAC, reached in the food box, and pulled out Spaghetti in Meat Sauce.

It could be worse, he thought.

The spaghetti was not too horrible, and Aiden rather liked the Cherry Blueberry Cobbler. There just wasn't enough of it.

He made his way to the table the team had staked out. About half of the guys were there, and he plopped down beside Cree, who as usual, was arguing football, this time with Brett. Cree gave him a nod, but didn't stop his logic for why the Raiders would break through this year. The nod was a good sign, though. After yesterday, he had fully been integrated into the team. He was one of them.

He had barely gotten back into his uniform and battle gear when several of the team had come back down the trail looking for him. They were relieved to find him and pissed that he hadn't been answering the radio. He showed them the bent connector, glad he had thought of that. They rushed back to the rest of the team only to find out that the mission had been scrubbed. There were two of the mujahideen Aiden had killed on the trail. One was looking sort of smushed, but the other looked pretty torn up as well. He was probably the one that had been hit by the grenade, and then he'd been badly mangled by rocks on the way down. That body had

---

[21] MRE: Meal, Ready to Eat. This is a prepackaged meal that could be carried into the field.

actually hit Brett as it landed. It was a glancing blow on Brett's leg, and Doc was checking him out as Aiden came up. There was no sign of the third body.

Dave—Master Sergeant David Teller—the team chief, wanted to know what happened, so Aiden gave a very sanitized version of things. With the mangled body, Aiden said he'd shot the man first, and the Taliban had fallen off the cliff. He said he'd shot the man still up on the top as well as the missing mujahideen, and that in a struggle, he'd managed to push the third man over the edge.

That got the attention of the others within hearing. Then Norm—Captain Norman Hockstetter—the team leader, walked up, and Aiden had to start all over again.

Calling a Marine captain by his first name still seemed odd to him, but for members of MSOTs, that seemed to be SOP. There was no doubt that Norm was in command—it was just that instead of "Captain," he was "Norm."

The team had escaped serious injury. Javier had a badly broken finger, Brett was bruised, and both Jim and Kyong had taken some shrapnel from a grenade that had landed near them, but both were mobile and while pissed, were fine after Doc had been able to pull out the little bits of metal in their legs. A little closer, and the outcome for those two might not have been as favorable.

Doc spotted Aiden's punctured trou and the blood on them and asked him if he needed help. Aiden knew his body would be working furiously to heal him, pushing the shrapnel out of his flesh, and he didn't want Doc to see that. He told him that he'd just gotten a few scrapes on the rocks during his climb. Doc looked concerned, but he let it be.

If the Taliban on the other side had been able to get a little higher, their plunging fire would have wrecked havoc among the team, and they would not have been able to wait for air. They would have had to rush out of the kill zone, and more of them would undoubtedly have been killed or WIA.[22] The Taliban ambush had been well-planned, but the terrain, while favorable to the mujahideen, had not been perfect.

---

[22] WIA: Wounded In Action

With the surprise order to scrub the mission, Norm told Aiden's element to try and police up as many of the grenades he'd dropped as possible while Husni's—Staff Sergeant Husni Fawzi—element provided security. Aiden took some good-natured grief over dropping the grenades, and they were only able to find 15 of them. Aiden was sure there had at least been double that number, but that was the best they could do.

They were back at the FOB by evening, and then the debrief started. Norm was more than a little upset that no one seemed to know who scrubbed the mission or why. For Aiden, with hunger pangs shooting through him, he just wanted to get done with the debrief and out of there so he could eat. With that one-legged Army major and his one-legged assistant standing there silently listening in, of course it was Aiden's debrief that took the longest. The Army lieutenant actually doing the brief seemed barely older than Aiden, and he seemed dutifully impressed with what Aiden said, even if Aiden downplayed as much as he could.

After the debrief, Dave took him aside and said, "Norm told me he was going to put you in for another Bronze Star. That's a Silver Star and three Bronze Stars, all in three years? And I read your write up for the Navy Cross, the one that got downgraded to a Bronze Star. That probably should have been a Navy Cross, and for the life of me, I don't know what went on with that."

"It was no big deal, Dave," Aiden said, and he meant it. To be put in for an award for when he was a varg didn't seem right. He was far more proud of the Bronze Star he'd been awarded for taking out the Council enforcer Oleksander.

"The thing is, I spoke with Gunny Despirito back in your old unit when we got word you were coming."

That was a surprise to Aiden. What had his former gunny said about him? In the back of his mind, he noted that Dave referred to the other Marine as "Gunny." Aiden guessed that the MSOT habit of first names only worked within the team itself—elsewhere, Marine discipline still held sway.

"He told me you were a no-shit hard-ass, but kind of a cowboy, going off on your own. And today, what did you do? Run off alone."

Dave stood looking at him as if waiting for Aiden to respond.

"Are you a medal hound?" he asked Aiden, direct and to the point.

The question took Aiden by surprise. *A medal hound?* Not in the least.

"No, no way, Dave."

"We're a team here, and we need to be a team in order to be successful. We don't need any cowboys out shooting for glory, 'cause that's what gets people killed. *Comprende?*"

"Yeah, sure. I understand," he tried to reassure his team chief.

"So no more solo missions, right?"

"Of course, no solo missions."

Dave looked at him for a few heartbeats, then clapped him on the shoulder. "Good. Just getting that cleared up. Go get yourself some chow."

Aiden hurried off, shaken by Dave's little conversation. He was probably going to be watched closely when they went out again.

The next morning, after two MREs and a shower the night before, sleep, and then a chat with Claire after he woke up, Aiden was in a much better mood as he opened up his breakfast spaghetti meal, pulling out the cobbler and scarfing it down.

"Hey, your boyfriend's over there," Brett said to him, interrupting Cree.

Aiden looked up to see the Army major on the other side of the DFAC, looking at him. As their eyes met, the major quickly looked down at his meal.

"What the fuck, Brett? Boyfriend?" Aiden said sourly.

"Well, he sure as shit's got the hots for you," Brett insisted while Cree and Daron, sitting across the table from them, nodded,

"You know, don't ask don't tell," Daron, one of the team's communicators, said, holding up his hand to high-five Brett.

"Eat me," Aiden said, taking another bite of his cobbler.

"Oh, I'm sure he will, if you ask him," Brett barely got out past his attempt to hold in his laughter.

I walked into that one, Aiden thought.

The banter was all part of the game, and while it might not seem so to the uninitiated, it was just further proof that Aiden had been accepted. Cree tried to pull Brett back to the NFL as Aiden ate the last piece of cobbler.

He gave a quick glance back at the major. Brett's razzing aside, it really was a little creepy that the guy always seemed to be watching him.

Chapter 5

The next week was pretty quiet. The team went out on two interdiction missions where they were supposed to watch the trails for Taliban movement, and then call for air or attack if the numbers were favorable. Each time, they bypassed the main path to the next village, instead taking what were nothing more than goat trails that the terp[23] had found out about from a local (probably for a nice monetary reward).

Charlie Company, the Army unit at the FOB, made a patrol in force through the ambush site and to the village, but neither the company nor the team had any contact. There was some grumbling about that. The team had been in-country for almost two weeks, and except for Manny, Javier, and Aiden, none of them had done much other than be a target. All the members of the team joined for the action, and they were getting bored.

When not out beyond the wire, most of the team were anally diligent about maintaining their equipment. For the guys with comms, that seemed reasonable. But Griff constantly worked on their GMVs, even though they hadn't been driven since the team arrived at the FOB. Aiden could only clean his M4 so many times, so while Griff was out in their corner of the motor pool, Aiden had borrowed Griff's Kindle.

Aiden hadn't even heard of a Kindle, and he was amazed at the number of books and magazines Griff had downloaded into it before deploying. He had more in the little unit than all the books in the FOB "library," which consisted of a box with maybe 50 ratty books donated by the USO.

"Get yourselves ready to mount out!" Dave shouted as he came into their GP tent. "We've got a mission. Count on up to two days."

Aiden tossed the Kindle on Griff's cot and rushed to get his gear. Nothing had been planned for the afternoon, so this had to be

---

[23] Terp: slang for interpreter

a real-time development. Within two minutes, he had his gear on, ready to go. Unbeknownst to the rest, his battle kit had a few extra pieces of gear. In his assault pack were an extra frog and extra boots. No one in the team carried extra boots, as far as Aiden knew. They were just extra weight. But this was part of Aiden's werewolf kit. If he had to shift, he'd take the assault pack, and after shifting back, he'd be able to get back into a semblance of a uniform.

Norm came into the tent, calling them forward. "A French Rafael either crashed or was shot down in our AO. Drone surveillance shows an increase of Taliban activity, and the electronics chatter is pretty clear that the Taliban want the pilot. We're getting a 47[24] here to lift us near our best guesstimate of where he might be. Charlie Company will be sweeping the lower reaches while we have some of the more unreachable terrain. Husni and Mike, get your elements ready for at least two days before resupply, and remember, it might be plenty cold where we're going. Thiago and Dave, you come with me for our ops-order.[25] We're supposed to be ready to embark in 45."

Mike was SSgt Mike Gandy, Aiden's element leader. Thiago was GySgt Thiago Mendez, the operations chief.

The next 45 minutes went by in a rush. Norm came back after 20 minutes and gave them the ops-order, but it was not extremely detailed. Marines like to plan things out to a T, but this was one of those times when they had to react based on training.

Four big 47's arrived on station. The FOB's helo pad was not big enough for two at the same time, so the team was rushed onto their bird and sent on its way so Charlie could be embark on their birds.

Aiden didn't like the entire team being on one bird. Some of the most significant loss of life in the 'Stan, to include other operators,[26] was when 47's had been shot down. Spread-loading

---

[24] CH-47: A large, Army twin-rotor helicopter
[25] Op-order: Operations order. This is the plan for any operations and covers the situation, mission, the enemy situation, admin and logistics, and communication.
[26] Operators: Slang for various special forces personnel form all branches of the service.

among several birds was the preferred method, but this time, there was no getting around it.

The 47 was a powerful bird, and it could reach higher altitudes than most other helos. Within half an hour, the big bird was flaring in on a tiny rocky outcrop, its rear wheels on the mountain, its front hanging over a 100 meter drop. The team rushed out, and the helo lifted back off, ready to get more boots in the mountains to find the missing pilot.

After a few moments, the two elements broke up. Hosni's element, with Norm, started making its way to the last known position of the pilot's personal responder, which was near where surveillance drones had spotted a parachute. Mike's element, with Dave coming along, headed down the slope to where they had decided that the pilot, if he were mobile, would probably head.

The helo had let them off on a windswept rocky slope. Within a few hundred meters, though, Aiden's team reached the trees. The Hindu Kush forest was not the dense stands of trees that were in the Eastern US or in the Pacific Northwest. They were more like the eastern Sierras, scattered, but dense enough to cut down on visibility. They offered some cover, but moving among them was easy enough. Within 20 minutes, they had reached the depression where the pilot might have tried to walk himself out. It was also a logical terrain feature that the Taliban might use to try and reach the pilot, and each member of the element knew that.

The depression was in the shadows of the western peaks, and already, the temperature was dropping. Winter was still a long way off, but this high, when the sun went down, it could get cold. No one knew what the pilot had as far as clothing, but without shelter, he could be susceptible to hypothermia.

Mike's plan was to set them up in what was essentially a blocking position along the small draw that formed the depression. They would hold this position until Norm and Hosni's element arrived at their objective, a good klick up the depression. If the pilot came diddy-bopping down the trail, all the better. If the Taliban came, either up from below or down from the other element's direction, they would take whatever action was deemed necessary.

Just as darkness was falling, Norm got on the hook to tell them they had reached the parachute, but there was no sign of the pilot. After some discussion with Dave, he made the command decision to hold steady for the night. Even with NVDs[27], tramping around the mountain tops in the dark was an accident waiting to happen. Mike broke them down into two-man teams and spread them out perpendicular to the draw with half of the element uphill of it and the other half on the downhill side. Aiden and Larry—Sgt Laurent Januski, the element's operator/breacher—had the far left flank, the one lowest in elevation. The two Marines took cover behind a fallen tree trunk and settled for the night. Larry broke out an MRE, eating it cold, before pulling out his polypros[28] and putting them on. With Aiden taking the first watch, Larry leaned back against the tree, and within minutes, was out.

Aiden settled in for a long, cold night. Actually, the cold didn't bother him much at all. The boredom would be taxing, though, and with ten hours before dawn, he had five hours before he could wake up Larry and get some sleep himself. Aiden quietly munched on his MRE, senses on the alert for any sign of movement. While the pilot might stumble around, he doubted that the mujahideen would be up and moving about. They would understand the dangers of a misstep in the dark.

So Aiden was rather surprised when he heard the unmistakable sound of feet approaching somewhere in the trees and down the slope from him. He tried to discern who it might be. Twice he heard voices, but they were too far off and too faint for him to make out the language. Without his improved hearing, he doubted he would have heard anything at all.

Ever since his shift at the ambush, it was as if Aiden's body suddenly remembered what is was like to be in varg mode, and it seemed to him that every cell in his body cried out for more. He wanted to shift, but he had been warned against doing so. He needed an excuse to break that restriction. That excuse could be the

---

[27] NVD: Night Vision Device

[28] Polypros: polypropylene trousers and turtleneck designed to be worn under the digital cammies. These are also known as "silkweights."

small group of men somewhere up ahead and slightly down-slope of him.

I've got to check them out, right? he reasoned.

But Dave's admonition still resonated in his mind—no more cowboying!

Still, just seeing who was there was a recon, nothing more. It could be some goat farmers trying to get home, for all he knew. If it was Terry Taliban, he could alert the rest of the team.

He looked over at the sleeping Larry. He was tempted to just slip off, but that would leave Larry defenseless.

"Hey, Larry," he whispered, shaking the sergeant's shoulder.

"What, it's already time?" Larry answered grumpily.

"No, sorry, but I've got to take a wicked shit, man. I need you up while I do it."

"So take it," Larry said, pulling the e-tool off the side of his pack and shoving it along the ground to Aiden.

"Uh, I think it's going to be a bad one. My gut's on fire."

That caught Larry's attention. In the darkness, when sight was limited, the sense of smell was heightened. A pile of shit, even when covered, could pinpoint their position to any advancing mujahideen.

"You can't hold it" he asked.

"I've been trying to. I'm at my limit," Aiden told him.

"Fuck. OK, go ahead, then down the slope 10 or 15 meters. Dig the hole deep and make sure you cover it," Larry said.

With any mujahideen coming up from the west, it made sense for him to go to the east, in front of them, from where only the French pilot might approach them. Aiden took the e-tool, then moved off, making sure there were enough trees between him and Larry to hide him.

Once out of sight, he dropped his assault pack, tore off his boots and frog, then shifted. The world coalesced into an intense flow of smells and sounds. Immediately he swiveled to pinpoint the approaching men. He could hear four men walking, but two of them had deliberate footsteps, as if they were carrying something heavy. Two more seemed unburdened. There was another smell, that of a man, but different than the other four. It wasn't the blood that made him different, nor even the faint whiff of aviation fuel. He just had his own underlying odor. It could be the man's food, it could be genetics, but he was different, and Aiden was positive that this was the pilot.

The draw they were protecting came down alongside the mountain. On one side, the steep slope rose to the peak. On the other side, after passing the small lip of the draw, the mountain continued down until it reached some distant valley. Mike's element was closing off the draw as a route of movement, but there were only so many Marines in the element, and they could cover only so much. If someone crossed below the last two members—Aiden and Larry— he or she would be long gone and out in the vast Afghan wilderness.

Forgetting his plan to get the rest of the team involved, Aiden flowed through the trees like a wraith. Within moments, he could make out the group of men struggling along another goat path, one that the element didn't realize existed. One man was in the lead, his AK at the ready as he peered into the darkness. With his beard and turban, all Aiden could see of his face were his eyes.

Immediately behind him were two men carrying a poncho stretcher hung like a hammock from a sturdy branch, the ends of which rested on the shoulders of the two men. The poncho bulged with its cargo. Without a shred of doubt, Aiden knew this was the French pilot. Behind the two stretcher-bearers, another man followed, providing rear security. The rear man was small, and he moved with a sense of nervousness.

Aiden knew he should alert the element and let the entire team rescue the pilot. He should not be a cowboy. But if the element assaulted, the mujahideen would undoubtedly kill the pilot. They needed him alive for their propaganda videos, but a dead pilot was better than a rescued pilot.

In the far recesses of his mind, Aiden knew he was just fishing for an excuse. The fact was that his bloodlust was growing, and he wanted to attack. He *needed* to attack.

Without bothering to think things through, he launched himself the last 20 meters and collided with the point security. Aiden wasn't even sure if the man saw him at all. One moment, he

31

was carefully walking; the next moment, something big and angry crashed into him, a paw nearly knocking his head off of his body.

Aiden didn't bother to stop and admire his handiwork. The front man of the stretcher team saw the collision, and he dropped his end of the makeshift stretcher, reaching to pull around his AK from where he had slung it across his shoulder. Aiden didn't give him a chance. He sunk his teeth into the man's neck, reveling in the hot blood that gushed into his mouth. He swallowed, savoring the taste of life, of power, which was ironic as the taste of life was the sign of impending death for the Taliban fighter.

The staccato of AK fire next to his ears broke his concentration. The other stretcher bearer had gotten his AK slung and was firing as he gibbered mindlessly. The only word Aiden could clearly hear was "*shaytan*," the same word he'd heard back at the ambush site.

Aiden jumped over the prone pilot just at the man swung his AK up, and a round lanced through Aiden's left biceps. Aiden ignored the pain and tackled the man, landing astride his chest.

The man tried to crawl away, and as Aiden wasn't any heavier than he was in human form, the man was making good progress. Aiden reached forward and grabbed the mujahideen's head. His varg hands were not as dexterous as his human hands, but they were good enough. With a simple twist, the man's neck was broken.

Aiden wanted to howl in victory, but footsteps registered on his mind. The other man! When in varg form, his mind didn't seem as organized, and he'd forgotten the fourth mujahideen. Luckily, the man was not attacking, but was in full flight. Aiden jumped up to give chase. He couldn't let anyone get away.

The man was running blind, smacking into trees in his panic. Aiden caught the word "*shaytan*" again, as the man sobbed in fear. Aiden wondered what it meant as he closed the gap. The ill-fated man ran into one more tree and stumbled as Aiden reached him. Aiden grabbed the man by the back of the neck and slammed him back into the same tree. Another neck broke, and the man fell limp to the ground.

Only it wasn't a man, Aiden saw. It was only a boy, possibly 12 or 13 years old. Aiden had killed a child. He knew that would bother him later, but for the moment his human mind struggled to push through his varg bloodlust. Aiden knew he had to work quickly. The entire element would have heard the gunfire.

Aiden rush back to the three dead mujahideen and the hopefully alive pilot. The man was only half conscious, clearly hurt. Aiden took the point man's AK, propped the body up, then pulled back on the pilot's hand, firing a burst which hit the body in the torso, knocking it down. He fired another burst into the rear stretcher bearer as the pilot moaned.

The other stretcher bearer was more problematic. Aiden had torn out half of his throat. After only a momentary pause, he pulled a grenade off the old British cartridge belt one of the Taliban was wearing, pulled the pin, and placed it next to the neck of the body, right up against Aiden's teeth marks. The body should shield the pilot from the blast. He released the spoon and sprinted back to where he'd left his clothes. This time, he hadn't needed his "werewolf kit," as he struggled to get back in his gear. His arm hurt, but at least his frog covered the already-healing wound.

"Coming in," he hissed at Larry, buttoning up his trou as he did so.

"What the fuck, Aiden? Did you see anything?" Larry hissed.

"No," Aiden answered. "It was just beyond me. I had my trou around my ankles. I thought they were shooting at my ass!"

"What a time to take a dump!" Larry said. "Hold up for a minute. The rest of the team's coming in so we can investigate."

Within a few moments, ten Marines were ready to move out, with three more providing rear security. Aiden knew where they were going, but Mike led them a bit too far forward. Brett found the dead kid, though, and called the rest of the element in. Almost immediately, the rest of the muj and the pilot were spotted.

"Look at what that beast did," Cree said in awe as he took in the scene. "Half-dead, he zeroed their fucking asses!"

Mike had them do a sweep while Javier, who'd had first aid training and would fill in until Doc, who was with the other element, could get to the scene. Of course, nothing was found. Aiden had taken out the entire group. But he dutifully searched.

It was more than an hour before the other element and Norm arrived at their position. Doc examined the pilot, stating his amazement that this man, in this condition, had taken out three muj and scared another so bad that he had run into a tree and somehow killed himself.

Aiden was the butt of several jokes, all along the lines of "getting the shit scared out of him" when the firing opened up. He took is good-naturedly, but a part of him wanted to scream out that this was his victory. He didn't want the pilot to get credit for his kills. When Dave acknowledged that Aiden had "waited" for the rest of the element before investigating, Aiden didn't feel any guilt, and actually wanted to confess as to what he'd done. But he bit his tongue and resisted.

The entire team put a perimeter around the pilot. Any Taliban in the area would have heard the firefight, and they had to know that they'd probably lost their prisoner. The Marines had to be alert for a counterattack. But the night was quiet, and after another six hours, it was dawn. They moved the pilot up the slope to a field expedient LZ, and a 47 flew in to medivac the pilot and get the team out of the mountains and back to the FOB.

Chapter 6

Hozan threw the plastic bag into the dumpster. The morning meal was over, but there was no rest for the weary. Lunch prep was in full swing.

Hozan wasn't even sure why he was still working in the DFAC. He'd only taken the original position at Camp Fallujah in order to be close to the information he'd needed to take out Saddam Hussein. Then he'd gone to Ramadi to be closer to Aiden Kaas, the *kreuzeung*[29] with whom he been inexorably linked. Now, Aiden was off in Afghanistan, and Hozan should have returned to northern Iraq where most of his fellow Kurds lived. Instead, he was dishing out food at Camp Liberty outside of Baghdad. Soon, almost all of the Americans would be gone, and he'd have no more excuses not to go home to Halabja. Hozan was not a superstitious man—few of the Tribe were. But he did not look forward to greeting the ghosts of his family and friends in that unfortunate town.

He closed the lid on the dumpster and had just started to walk inside when an almost-smell hit him. One of the Tribe was here, he realized. He'd been picking up hints all night that another werewolf was in the area. That shouldn't be surprising. Baghdad was a big city, and the ebb and flow of people brought many to its stucco warrens. This was different. Someone was close and approaching him with a sense of purpose. Hozan didn't know who it was, so he simply stood by the dumpsters and waited. He'd know soon enough.

Hozan didn't know how he could sense the others in the Tribe so easily. Not many others could. It wasn't a sense of smell, actually, even if that might be the closest analogy. It was sort of a tickle in his mind that told him others were in the area.

When the Arab emerged from the buildings some five minutes later, Hozan immediately knew this was his target. The man looked

---

[29] Kreuzeung: a werewolf who has been turned as opposed to a "blood," or one born into the tribe.

to be about 60, which for a werewolf, might mean anywhere from 80 to 90 years old. He was in full Arab dress, his *thwab* white and his *keffiyeh* red and white checked.

He scanned the area, and when his eyes finally locked on Hozan's he purposely strode over.

"*As-salaam 'alaykum*, Hozan Kamaran Mardin," the man said, holding out his hand.

As soon as he heard the voice, Hozan knew who this visitor was. He'd talked with the man on the phone before, and he had a good memory for voices. What he didn't understand is why the esteemed Nemir Muhmood, a member of the tribal council, had left Germany to come back to Iraq and find him.

"*As-salaam 'alaykum, Nemir Muhmood,*" he replied, offering nothing else.

Nemir was the father of Omar Muhmood, Aiden's patron. Aiden had called Nemir when Losenko had been sent to kill Aiden and begged Nemir to recall the assassin. That Losenko was there had been a surprise to Nemir. The assassin had been sent without authorization by Günter Wais, another rival council member.

Hozan stared passively at the man, waiting. His heart gave a few extra beats, though, as he wondered why the visit. Had the Council finally decided to rid themselves of their unauthorized kreuzeung?

Finally, Nemir broke the silence with, "Your ward has been active in Afghanistan."

Ward?

Technically, Aiden was not Hozan's ward. The dead Omar, Nemir's son was Aiden's patron, so Aiden was Omar's ward. But Hozan had nursed Aiden through his first shift, he has taught Aiden about the ways of the Tribe. So if this orphan had a ward, Hozan would take up the title.

"Active?" he asked, leaving it at that.

"Yes. Active. He has shifted twice now in advancing the cause of the humans."

Hozan's heart fell. He'd warned the headstrong young man about shifting, and he'd thought the warning had taken root. To shift to advance one of the causes of man was *verboten*. It could bring unwanted attention onto the Tribe.

His thoughts darted around his brain like a songbird in a cage. He tried to think up an excuse.

"You know the rumors as well as I do, about feral tribes who inhabit the Afghan and Pakistani mountains. It could have been them," he argued.

"They are not mere rumors, but no, this was your ward," Nemir said, offering no room for argument.

Hozan's heart fell. He'd been ready to kill Aiden after he'd been infected. But over time, he'd grown very fond of the boy. Hozan knew that could be a reaction to losing his entire family to Saddam's gas, but reaction or not, the feelings were real. And he would not—no, could not—carry out any orders to execute him.

Something seemed to flicker in the council member's eyes, and he seemed to deflate a fraction as he stood there.

"I need you to go to him," Nemir said. "Make him listen to you. I've arranged for you to be transferred to the cafeteria where Aiden is stationed. Talk to him. Get him to hold off on shifting. I can only do so much to keep him alive, and he's not making it any easier for me."

Hozan stared at Nemir in surprise. He was going to Afghanistan? To be close to Aiden? He needed to know why. He thought he knew, but he wanted it out in the open.

"Why?" was all he asked.

Tears welled up in Nemir's eyes. "When I lost Omar, I lost my family. And Omar was, well, I am sure you heard. He hated humans with a passion, and he casually used them as prey, I know. But he was my son, my only son. And when Aiden Kaas took his seed and survived, he kept part of Omar alive. As long as Aiden is alive, my Omar is alive, too."

Hozan understood Nemir, to his great sorrow. He'd lost his entire family when Hussein had gassed his town. Everyone. This sorrow, this anguish, was something, as bad as it was, that he could trust. This was not some political game, some struggle for power. This was a heartbroken man crying out for help, and that assistance

Jonathan P. Brazee

coincided with Hozan's own wishes. Aiden was Hozan's ward, no less than if it had been his seed that had initiated the change in him.

He took Nemir's arm in the old way, forearm to forearm, hand grasping just short of the elbow.

"I would be proud to undertake this task."

Chapter 7

Qalandar stood in front of Zakia, waiting for an answer. He'd brought along several of his cronies for support, all older members of the tribe. This was a public discussion, though, so most of the rest of the tribe were gathered around, waiting as well for her to make a decision.

The unknown werewolf had struck again, killing four men on the slopes of a nearby mountain. Once again, the dead men came from the Taliban sect, and while Zakia had no love lost for them, they could be dogged in their pursuit of protecting their drug trade, driven by both greed and religious fervor. Zakia's people had suffered from these men's forefathers, and she had little doubt that should the Taliban become aware of this enclave of the Tribe, they would stop at nothing to eradicate them.

Their kind was considered *haram*, or "forbidden," to the people who shared their mountains. They still survived by hiding, by keeping out of sight and mind. Zakia knew that the rumors of members of the Tribe roaming the mountains kept most of the humans at bay, afraid of the creatures of the night. The smugglers, however, would not be afraid. If they knew of the *Leewekhel*, her small tribe hidden in the mountains, they would close in and destroy them. Their tribe even hid from the *Tribe*. Zakia knew the other werewolves had some sort of organization out beyond her mountains, but they were foreigners, too, not to be trusted any more than the humans.

Now it looked like one of them had moved into their area and was attacking the Taliban smugglers. That threatened to expose their village, to put them at risk, and that could not be allowed to happen. Qalandar wanted action, and Zakia was in full compliance. There was only one choice.

The tribe had to act to protect itself.

Chapter 8

Aiden waited in the chow line. It was hot-meal time, and while he'd essentially recovered from his shifting and healing, he still had a bigger appetite than most of his fellow Marines and soldiers. The hot chow here was not as good as what they'd had in Fallujah and Ramadi, not as good as at Camp Leatherneck, but still, it was better than MREs.

"Good evening, Cpl Kaas," the server said as Aiden made it to the front of the line.

Aiden looked up in shock. Standing in front of him, ready to dish up his choice of potatoes or rice, was Hozan.

"Hozan! What're you doing here?" he stammered out.

"I've been transferred here. It is good to see you again. Perhaps we can catch up later?" Hozan asked before turning to the next Marine and asking him what he wanted.

Aiden stumbled to the next station, getting chili ladled over the rice Hozan had given him. He kept glancing back at Hozan, who was now ignoring him. In a daze, Aiden got the rest of his food and made his way to the team's table.

"You know that hajji?" Griff asked as he sat down beside him. "We weren't at Leatherneck long enough for introductions."

"No. I mean no, I didn't meet him at Leatherneck. He's Iraqi, a Kurd. I met him at Hurricane Point," he said, not bothering to tell Griff that Hozan had followed him to the Ramadi base after Aiden had first met him at Fallujah. "He used to hook us up with extra chow. You can ask Doc."

Aiden doubted that Doc would remember Hozan, but he panicked just a little and wanted to deflect the attention from Hozan and him. He needn't have worried.

"Ah, OK, good shit. Maybe he can hook us up here, too. Check it out for us, OK?"

"Sure, no problem."

The rest of the meal went by in a blur. He didn't remember eating, but when he returned his tray, his plate was clean, so he must have downed the chow. He went back to their tent, and with nervous energy, cleaned his M4 one more time. The rest of the team wandered in; some lying down for a nap, another group starting a game of poker. The team was scheduled to go out on a mission later that night, so they had a few hours of free time.

Aiden waited an hour, then made his way back to the DFAC. He sat on the crude wooden bench left by a previous unit at the FOB.

Why is Hozan here? he wondered. He knew this was not a mere coincidence.

He waited another 30 minutes before Hozan came from around the back of the DFAC. Aiden stood up, and both men hugged each other. Aiden didn't know why Hozan was there, but he was glad to see his friend.

"What . . . how?" he started.

"You've shifted," Hozan simply said.

"Well, yeah. But what good is it to be a werewolf if you never shift? And I had to; it was an emergency."

"The Council has noted it, even out here in these mountains. And you are shifting in support of man, which is forbidden."

"This is my team, Hozan. And I have to do what I have to do to protect them," Aiden said. "Besides, when you were a Peshmerga, didn't you ever shift?"

Hozan had the grace to look embarrassed. "Yes, I did, on several occasions. But I am of the blood, and you are *kreuzung*," he said, holding up a hand to stop Aiden's protest. "I am not saying I am more worthy. I'm just stating the facts. And even as a *kreuzung*, you were not an authorized infection. There are factions within the Council that want you dead, and they will seize any opportunity to make it so."

"And so why are you here?" Aiden asked, his stomach turning sour as he heard Hozan's words.

"Others want you left alone, such as Nemir Muhmood."

"The father of Omar, the guy who turned me?"

"Yes. He has taken an interest in you, and he sent me here so I can offer my guidance to you."

"So you are here to babysit me?"

Hozan gave a half shrug.

"Look, Hozan, I'm glad to see you. Really glad. And I'll try to be good. But if I need to shift to keep my team alive, then I will, and the Council can kiss my ass. If they want to come for me, they'll know where to find me. Last time that happened, it didn't work out so well for them."

Aiden was speaking with a sense of bravado that wasn't totally genuine. He knew he'd been unbelievably lucky with Oleksander. Before that, in the desert outside of Las Vegas, he'd been beaten pretty handily by two American werewolves. Like it or not, he was a *kreuzung* and not as powerful as a blood.

On the other hand, he'd about had it with this almighty Council. He'd never asked to be turned. And now they seemed to have the power to decide if he was good enough just to live. He'd never met any of them, and they'd never met him, so by what right did they get to decide his fate?

Let the fuckers come, he thought to himself. *If they are man enough—no, werewolf enough—to come after me, I'll make that a very painful evolution.*

I'm a Marine, and we're a harder out than anyone else walking the planet.

Chapter 9

The team was broken into its two elements. Each one had eyes on a trail leading through the mountains. "Trail" might have been an overstatement, though. A rabbit would have had a hard time using it. Evidently, though, the Taliban thought it was a highway—at least according to their source.

Supposedly, a small smuggling team was going to come through the area in the early hours of the morning, and the team was positioned to interdict them. Stopping the flow of drugs, which funded the Taliban, was one of the team's primary missions. This would be their fifth such operation—each of the previous four came up empty.

They knew the drugs came through, as well as weapons and fighters who had rested up and trained in Pakistan. Every kilo of heroin, every RPG, every rested fighter who made it through had the potential to fund or fight the Coalition troops. Each Marine in the team wanted the mujahideen to try them. They wanted to do something positive for the overall mission in the country.

Hidden in the trees and rocks above the tiny trail, the Marines settled in to wait. It would not be dawn for another six hours or so, and they didn't expect anyone until then at the earliest. Down in the deserts, the mujahideen tried to make use of the night. In the mountains, that was quite a bit more dangerous.

Just a few meters away, Cree was lying prone alongside a big boulder. Aiden knew he was there, but he couldn't see him. He was tempted to try and shift only his nose to see if he could smell the other Marine, but he wasn't sure just how to do that. A finger shift alone was fairly easy for him now; however, trying a nose and olfactory system was beyond him, at least at the present time.

He'd been contemplating how to do that when he sensed something behind him. He didn't hear anything, he didn't see anything, he didn't smell anything. But he was positive that

43

something or things were out there. It didn't have the feeling of the Taliban, but there was a sense of danger. Like a Siren, it called him.

Aiden peered over to his right, trying to pierce the darkness and see Cree. He flipped down his NVDs, and still Cree was out of sight. Good. That meant he should be out of sight to Cree as well.

Despite his promise to Hozan not to shift unless absolutely necessary, Aiden took off his frog and helmet, unfastened his flak jacket, and shifted. Immediately, the richness of the night aromas assaulted his nose. The smell that demanded the most attention resonated within his body. It was werewolf.

Back there, maybe 30 or 40 meters, a pack of werewolves stood in the trees. He could smell their nervousness, their anger, and a sense of excitement. He couldn't tell how many there were, but certainly more than a few. There was something else, though. It was werewolf, but more: a deeper, more concentrated smell. It was as if some paranormal chef had taken *Essence of Werewolf* and reduced it to a more concentrated flavor. What was freakier, to Aiden's senses, was that this concentrated odor reeked of, not exactly sexuality, but a compulsion that had to tickle the same part of the brain as where the sexual drive formed. He had to find the source of that smell.

With nary a thought for the team, Aiden flowed back through the trees, a wraith in the night. Within moments, other werewolves materialized out of the trees to quietly surround him. Aiden had brought his M4, and he felt the animosity of the other werewolves, but he did not engage them. The concentrated sense called to him.

Then she stepped out of the shadows. Aiden immediately knew that she was the source of the smell. What shocked Aiden was that she was a huge, silver wolf. Not a werewolf, but an honest-to-goodness wolf.

The big wolf padded up to him, then stared into his eyes. Aiden had always heard that animals could not meet a human's eyes. That obviously did not pertain to wolves as it was Aiden who broke contact. She turned and started walking off. Somehow, Aiden knew he was supposed to follow her. If he hadn't known, he would have guessed pretty quickly as the other werewolves, the ones like Aiden, started closing in on his side—whether an honor guard or an execution escort, he didn't know. There were 12 of them, and Aiden knew he couldn't take on that number. He wasn't sure he'd want to, anyway. He was anxious to find out more about the wolf, and following her seemed to be the most logical option.

The wolf broke out into a run, and Aiden had to work hard to keep up. He was getting winded when she stopped in what looked to be a natural amphitheater in the rocks and spun to face him. Aiden wasn't sure how far they'd run. He knew he should be with his team, and leaving them could have severe consequences, but it was almost as if his will was not his own.

The rest of the vargs were gathered in the amphitheater, surrounding the two of them. Aiden thought they had a more aggressive air about them.

The wolf stalked up to Aiden and stared once more into his eyes. Then with a flicker, she shifted into a werewolf. Immediately, the feeling of compulsion disappeared as Aiden stepped back in shock.

A wolf-werewolf?

The other werewolves crowded up closer, a blood lust beginning to permeate the air. Aiden started looking for an escape route, but nothing was evident.

The wolf-slash-werewolf put her muzzle just inches from Aiden's and said something that sounded like Pashto. Aiden hadn't learned more than a few words and phrases of the language as of yet.

"Za na poheegum," he said, meaning "I don't understand."

She switched to another language, one Aiden didn't recognize as anything he'd heard before.

"I don't understand you," he said, this time in English.

She seemed puzzled and looked around at the other werewolves. One stepped forward and approached them.

"You are British?" he asked.

"No, American," the wary Aiden answered.

"American?" the werewolf asked, obviously confused.

"Yes. American. USA, you know?"

Aiden found himself thinking that the werewolf did not know.

What century have I landed in? he wondered as the varg spoke to the leader, the one who had been a freaking wolf.

Several of the others got into it, holding what sounded to be a spirited conversation. Aiden understood none of it. With his lack of Pashto and the werewolves' less-than-articulate enunciation, it was beyond him. The vibe was not good, though, and he nervously fingered the trigger on his M4. The weapon probably wouldn't do much good against so many werewolves, though. He wished he had something with more punch with him.

Finally, it seemed like some sort of decision was made—and not a good one for Aiden. The pack's attention focused laser-like on him, and almost as one, they stepped forward. Aiden lowered his M4 and aimed it at them. Backwards or not, they had to recognize a rifle.

The queen bee shifted back to wolf form, and immediately Aiden felt his resolve start to melt. He forced himself to focus. He didn't know what he'd done to earn their ire, but if he was going to go, he'd be damned if he wouldn't take some of them with him. His own throaty growl joined the chorus from the others.

When the other wolf burst on the scene, Aiden almost shot it. But it jumped in front of Aiden and then turned to face the others, pure evil intent emanating from deep within its throat. The werewolves stopped in their tracks, suddenly unsure.

The ragged brown wolf slowly turned its head to glare at the queen wolf, completely ignoring Aiden. The pressure that hammered at Aiden's will faded. He had no idea who or what this wolf was, but it was keeping the others at bay. Aiden took a step closer to the brown wolf, weapon swiveling to cover the rest.

The two wolves faced each other down, then as some unknown signal to Aiden, shifted into vargs. Suddenly, it became clear to Aiden. He recognized the brown werewolf standing in front of him. Hozan had come to his rescue.

Only, it didn't seem to be a done deal.

The queen tried speaking to Hozan in Pashto, which Hozan didn't seem to understand. Hozan tried Kurdish, then Arabic, and while the female varg was able to repeat some of the Arabic words, it was evident to Aiden that she really wasn't fluent in the language.

She tried one more, and to Aiden's relief, Hozan seemed to understand it.

The two conversed, sometimes heatedly, while Aiden kept his weapon ready to engage any of the others. None of them seemed to be ready to attack, though. The bloodlust that Aiden had sensed before had faded, and now they seemed willing to let Hozan and their leader figure out what was going to happen.

At last, some sort of decision seemed to be reached. The other werewolves turned and started to move off.

Hozan leaned over and quietly said, "We are going with them. Put your rifle up and try to hold back any aggression."

"I can't go. My team is back there somewhere, and I've got to get back," he protested.

"You are going, or you are dead. I was able to convince her to delay any action, but you are not saved yet. We are going to their village now," Hozan said in a brook-no-argument tone.

"To their village? Don't Muslims have to treat visitors as guests?" Aiden asked.

"That, or kill them so they can't give the village's location away," was the curt reply.

"How long will this take? I've got to get back."

"It will take as long as it takes."

They sped up into a steady run that effectively kept the two from talking. Aiden had a thousand more questions, not the least being what the fuck with the wolf thing? Aiden thought he'd grasped just what it meant to be a werewolf, but now that had been turned upside down again.

They ran in silence for almost 20 minutes before entering a tiny box canyon high in the mountains. Small houses hugged the rock walls, and a spring bubbled up from the cliff face and formed a pool in the center of the village. It seemed that most of the village, possibly 60 people, were up and waiting for the group to return. If they were surprised at two more vargs showing up, they didn't show it.

As the group came to a halt, the others shifted back to human. All of them were naked, including their leader, a 40-ish-looking woman. Seeing naked Afghans was odd, especially females, but none of them seemed the least bit embarrassed.

"Shift," Hozan hissed at him.

Aiden quickly shifted back to human as the others were handed their *khet partug*. Hozan was handed the typical Pashtun clothing as well. Within a few moments, several of the older men were seated on the ground with their leader, and Hozan and Aiden were offered seats. It seemed odd that their village head was a woman. Aiden had never heard of that in Afghanistan, but there was no mistaking that she was the top dog in the village.

Shomleh was served, and to Aiden's surprise, he liked it. He'd learned of it back during one of their pre-deployment briefs, but this was his first time to taste the minty yogurt drink.

He tried to will whatever was going to happen to happen quicker. He was probably 40 minutes or more from his team, and he had to get back before anyone missed him. Luckily, they would be lying as motionless as possible so as not to give out their position, but that wouldn't last forever.

Hozan did all the speaking, at least from what Aiden realized was "their side." It seemed surreal that while sitting there in the dark around a small fire, sipping yogurt, his fate was being decided. His fate and Hozan's he realized. If they decided against Aiden, then Hozan could not be allowed to leave, either.

There was none of the intensity as when the two were going at it back in the amphitheater. Now, one would say something, sip some *shomleh*, then listen as the other offered something back. Once in awhile, one of the older men would interject something. Aiden desperately wished he could understand what was being said. He wished he could speak up for himself.

Aiden was about to explode when finally, everyone stood up. Smiles were evident, and Aiden felt a surge of relief. A few of the older men came up and shook his hand, western style. They chattered away in Pashto, and Aiden nodded and smiled back. He didn't shake the leader's hand. Head of a village or not, it had been drilled into them by the Corps that you didn't shake a woman's hand in the 'Stan, and now that they were seemingly about to be let go, he didn't want to enrage anyone with a cultural faux pas.

It took at least 15 agonizingly slow minutes while farewells were made. With one last wave, the two men shifted, and with Hozan leading, the two vargs ran through the forests and back to the team. After 35 minutes, they stopped less than 500 meters from the ambush site.

"I will talk to you when you get back," Hozan said as he turned to run back to the FOB.

"What about the full wolf shift," Aiden asked, still burning with questions.

"Later," Hozan said as he ran off.

Aiden watched him for a few moments, then started to swing around to come up into the team. It wouldn't do to get caught coming back. He stayed in varg form and slowly slipped back into position. He could sense Cree over to his right, awake and alert. He shifted back and put back on his clothing and gear.

The night had been totally unexpected, and Aiden had to digest what had happened. But he needed more information from Hozan on just what the fuck that was all about. Hozan had almost assuredly saved his life, but he had a lot to answer.

Within an hour, dawn started lightening up the sky. Even in human form, Aiden could almost feel the tension in the air as the Marines waited for the muj to show up. That faded when by another three hours, nothing had happened. The intel was probably wrong again. They would have to stay in position until nightfall before extracting. They didn't want any observers to know they knew about this trail complex.

At about 0900, Mike crept down the line, checking on everyone with hand and arm signals. Aiden gave him a thumbs up then reverted back to his thoughts.

Thirty minutes later, the mountainside 500 meters away opened up with the sound of gunfire. Hosni's element was in contact. The fire intensified, then started to die off. Aiden wanted to know what was happening, but they had to maintain their position and in silence.

The firing up ahead stopped. Well, they wouldn't be staying until nightfall now, Aiden knew. Their position was blown. He started to relax when the SAW opened up 40 meters away from him.

Aiden swung his own M4 around to cover the trail as most of the rest of the element opened fire.

Aiden couldn't see anything, and he rose up to give himself a better view, but the trail directly below his position was empty. The fighting was at the other end of the element's ambush site.

"Cease fire," was passed over the net, the first time since they'd arrived that a word was spoken.

Aiden waited for orders but kept his eyes open for anything from below them. Three mujahideen were lying dead in their kill zone. Two were carrying packs filled with opium. Up with Hosni's team, five had been killed and one was slightly wounded and now a PUC.[30] Two of them had been opium mules, the other three fighters. This had been a righteous ambush.

Their position was too rugged for helos, so they were going to have to hump it out just as they had humped it in, but this time carrying almost 120 kilos of raw opium. Aiden was given one of the mujahideen packs.

From human to werewolf and now to opium mule, this had been an amazing 18 hours.

---

[30] PUC: Person Under Control—a term adopted to take the place of POW. If they were POWs they would have to be accorded certain treatment standards as required by the Geneva Convention.

Chapter 10

Rustam Nabiyev surveyed the scene, taking deep drafts of the mountain air into his lungs. He could pick up the faint odor of gunpowder. This was the spot where the group had been hit. Besides the odor, the dirt of the trail was still stained with blood, and some of the rocks and tree trunks around it showed signs of fighting. Rustam had lost 120 kilos of opium here, and he had to find out why.

To be more precise, the opium hadn't belonged to Rustam, but to Nikolai Borisov, his boss, who was sitting back in his guarded estate on the outskirts of Samarkand. Nikolai did not know of the lost shipment yet, but he would soon enough, and he would not take kindly to it, and the blame would fall squarely onto Rustam's shoulders. This was something Rustam desperately wanted to avoid. Getting onto Nikolai's bad side was not conducive to a long and happy life.

His guide, a Pathan[31] from the local village, was acting like he could actually glean some information from the ambush site. These mountain primitives were worthless other than as mules, no matter what side of the Afghan-Pakistani border they lived. Rustam was angry at the loss, angry that he would have to inform Nikolai that the shipment was gone. He wanted to take out that anger on the fool who was trying to act as if he could actually decipher the scene. He wondered if the man knew how close he was to dying right then and there. But Rustam was practical, if nothing else, and these mountain villagers had their pride and misplaced sense of honor. If Rustam needed their help in the future, then this idiot would have to get back to his hovel and wrinkled wife unharmed.

---

[31] Pathan: A term used by foreigners to identify Pashtun people. It is usually considered derogatory.

Rustam needed some privacy, though, if he was going to be able to find out who was responsible for this mess. He had to deflect Nikolai's anger to someone, anyone else.

"Where was the first site?" he asked in accentless Pashto.

"Up there," the old man said while pointing.

"I want you to see what you can find there. Meet me back here when you have something to tell me."

He watched the useless man move off. He was chattel, nothing more, but Rustam had to control himself. He couldn't let anger blind him.

When the man was well out of sight, Rustam let his pent-up anxiety speed his release as he shifted. For once, he appreciated the drab, loose Pashtun *khet partug* he had donned. While the traditional Uzbek *ishton*, with its wide legs and narrow ankles were suited to a shifting varg, the *kulyak* he normally wore could not be worn during a shift without being destroyed.

His pitiful human nose had only been able to pick up the faint whiff of gunpowder, but as a varg, it was as if a symphony of smell had sprung up around him. There was the blood in the dirt, the smell of urine, the smell of death. There were the smells of humans all around. He suddenly swung his head up as it hit him. It was unmistakable. It was varg, and more than that, it was lycan. A very powerful alpha lycan.

This put the incident into another realm, and one that might deflect Nikolai's anger from him. There were rumors of ferals in these mountains, and it looked as if the rumors were not only true, but that these ferals were trying to take over Nikolai's operations.

They would regret that. No one took on Nikolai and lived to tell about it. At least two other members of the Council had tried to take him on over the years, and both had conveniently disappeared. No dirty little feral tribe could hope to do any better.

For a moment, Rustam considered going after the tribe himself and recover the opium before Nikolai found out it had been taken in the first place. He could gather up a small army of Taliban. The idiots were easy to rile up, and all he had to do was to tell them that a tribe of *harram* werewolves were up there, and they would launch themselves in a religious frenzy in their efforts to eradicate the devil creatures. The irony that Rustam himself was such a "devil creature" was not lost on him.

He discarded that idea, though. Backwards little village or not, they could defeat a Taliban force, and then Nikolai would want to know why he hadn't been told immediately. No, it was better to tell Nikolai now and let him take care of the little alpha and her feral pack.

He sniffed the air deeply, getting a bearing on which direction the ferals had taken to leave the ambush site.

Run, little feral cousins, run! Nikolai is coming!

Chapter 11

Getting some privacy anywhere in the FOB was pretty difficult. It was a small area and pretty packed with people and equipment. There was the entire Charlie Company and assorted support staff. There was a platoon of the ANA[32], which didn't make the soldiers and Marines too happy, given the recent spate of green-on-blue[33] attacks. A squad of ANP[34] rotated in and out of the FOB. Then there were the various hangers-on whose job Aiden didn't know nor really care, the civilian contract workers, and the MSOT.

There was nothing wrong with Aiden talking to Hozan, but still, neither one of them wanted to be completely open about it; however, attempting to hide and then getting caught would raise more flags. They finally settled for the motor pool, by the team's GMVs.

Aiden immediately wanted to know about the entire wolf thing, the honest-to-goodness wolf thing, but Hozan pushed that aside for the moment, saying he would get back to it. First, he had to tell Aiden how close he'd been to getting himself killed.

The Leewekhel tribe was feral, not within the control of the Council. They weren't really feral as Hozan had previously described the term to Aiden. They hadn't reverted to a more animalistic mindset—they merely had opted out of the Tribe. They were well aware of the Tribe and its governing body, but they just chose to fade back into the mountains and live their lives as they would. As such, they wanted nothing to bring any attention on them, whether from the Council, the Taliban, the Afghan government, or the *parangay*. They were not aware of the Coalition or even the Soviet occupation before—to them, the *parangay* were

---

[32] ANA: Afghan National Army
[33] Green-on-Blue: Slang for attacks made by the ANA on Coalition personnel.
[34] ANP: Afghan National Police

the British, which was why they had't reacted to Aiden's claim of being an American.

There were always rumors of feral tribes (the Council considered anyone not under its control "feral") in the more remote areas of the world. Twenty years before, the Council had even acted on a small feral tribe living in northern Canada. That small group rejected the Council's authority and reverted to considering humans as nothing more than prey. The Council, fearful of exposure, eliminated the threat. So, according to Hozan, the Leewekhel might have good reason to stay out of sight.

Hozan had felt the shift of so many vargs and attuned his senses to the mountains above the FOB. When Aiden had shifted, he recognized it and shifted to his lycan form, that of a full wolf. He tore up the mountains, tracking the group down, hoping he would be in time. It had been a near thing. Another five minutes would have been too late, and Aiden would have been executed to keep the village's very existence a secret by eliminating any attention Aiden's shifting could bring to the area.

Hozan had burst into the village, where werewolf tradition going back hundreds of years gave him the right to speak. Unfortunately, Hozan did not speak Pashto, and no one in the tribe spoke Kurdish or Arabic, and only one oldster spoke any English. They finally found a common tongue: Farsi. It had taken awhile, but Hozan had finally convinced Zakia, their leader, that not only was Aiden not a threat, he was an ally. He was working to free the land of the drug smugglers, and any indiscretions he had shown while shifting were simply due to his only recently being turned and not knowing there was anyone else in the Tribe (the Leewekhel considered themselves as in the Tribe, just not under the Council) in the area.

To Aiden, Hozan's reasoning didn't make sense, but he was glad this Zakia accepted it. The alternative would not have boded well for either of the two of them.

Hozan had promised them that with Aiden's "high" position, he could help deflect attention from their tribe.

"My 'high position?'" Aiden had asked. "I'm a dumb grunt, nothing more. You lied to them."

"So you wanted me to tell the truth, that their fears were valid and they should kill us?" Hozan asked.

"No, of course not. It's just that I thought, I mean, you have your honor, right?"

"My honor died with my family in Halabja. My honor died when the Soviets used our Republic of Mahabad for their cold war propaganda, then turned us out when we were of no more use to them. My honor died when Günter Wais sent his assassin to kill you because he was at odds with your patron's father."

That shut Aiden up. And if that lie kept both of them alive, he was glad his friend had had the quick wits to make it. It wasn't as if Hozan had been completely honest with him, after all. He'd kept the entire wolf capability a secret from him.

Aiden was a little pissed about that, but also excited. He wanted to know more. At last, Hozan seemed finished with what happened in the village, and Aiden waited expectantly. He'd figured out the important part, but he wanted Hozan to confirm it.

When Hozan explained that while the varg form was the one most used by members of the Tribe, the lycan form was considered the pinnacle of their very essence. This is who they truly are.

"I knew it!" Aiden said. "So how can I make that shift?"

"You can't," Hozan said with a resigned expression.

"What, more Council rules? You know what they can do with those," Aiden said, suddenly angry.

"No, not the Council. Nature. Only bloods can make the full shift, and not every blood can do it. Kreuzung don't have the ability."

"Bullshit. You're lying again."

"I'm afraid that's the truth. You can try if you want, but you won't be able to do it. No kreuzung has ever made the shift."

Fuck yeah I'm going to try it. No, not just try it. Do it! Aiden thought.

Aiden grilled Hozan about the process, and his friend didn't seem to be holding back. Aiden was convinced that Hozan thought he was telling the truth. Aiden just didn't accept that as a fact.

One aspect about his experience with Zakia still confused him. It was her ability at thought control. Hozan always held that the

Tribe's abilities were based on science and nature, and thought control was right out of science fiction.

Hozan laughed when Aiden mentioned "mind control."

"No, it is nature. All members of the Tribe both give off and are susceptible—that is the word, right? Susceptible. Yes, all members are susceptible to pheromones. As a human, you can only barely sense them. As a varg, they are much more pronounced. And as a lycan, they can almost overwhelm you."

"But I felt her. I had to do what she wanted."

"Zakia is an alpha, a very strong alpha. That is why she is the leader."

"I wanted to ask you about that. Why is she the tribal chief? I thought only men held those positions here."

"Like I said, she is an alpha, and our biology has been developed over tens if not hundreds of thousands of years, long before human culture emerged. And she is an alpha because her pheromones are stronger than that of anyone else in her village. What you did was not what she wanted, really, but what you thought you wanted. You naturally felt subservient to her as an alpha, and you needed to let her know you accepted your positions relative to each other. She couldn't control you, but she could make you want to please her."

"That sounds pretty weird, if you ask me. It felt like mind control. I know about pheromone perfume and stuff, but when Claire tried it, I couldn't tell the difference," Aiden said, not convinced.

"But when your Claire wants you to bed her, you do, right?"

"Well yeah, of course. But that's just being in love."

"And is that all?"

"Well, horny, too," Aiden admitted, feeling uncomfortable discussing his sex life.

"Was your Claire using mind control?"

"No, of course not. I wanted it, too."

"And somehow, you knew she wanted you just like you wanted her. Pheromones," Hozan said smugly, point made.

Aiden gave up. He wasn't sure he bought all of that. Sometimes, despite their time together, Aiden still thought of Hozan as some backwards mountain Kurd, yet here he was talking about pheromones and pack alphas, things that were beyond Aiden's comprehension. Aiden had a lot to absorb, and it would take some thinking to get it all straight in his mind.

One thing was for sure, though. Hozan might be the werewolf expert, but not the Aiden expert. No matter what anyone else thought, Aiden *would* make the shift all the way to his inner wolf.

Chapter 12

"He'll be here in a few minutes," MT said, coming in the little plywood structure that stood in as Keenan's "office."

Keenan sat behind his field desk, marshalling his thoughts. He needed some feedback from MT.

"So, what do you think?" he asked his assistant.

"Think about what?" MT asked.

"You know damned well what. About our little call," Keenan said.

"I . . . uh . . . I don't think that's my call."

"Bullshit. I want your opinion. Was the colonel involved with this little incident?"

MT looked pensive, as if trying to figure out what he could and could not say. Keenan and MT had a very close working relationship that went beyond them both missing legs, and they tended to be quite informal with each other. But still, Keenan was a major, MT a Spec 5, and they were discussing a bird colonel.

"If you really want to know my opinion," he finally relented, "I think it smells like shit."

Which was exactly what Keenan thought, if not so eloquently put. During their phone update, Colonel Tarniton had berated Keenan for his lack of progress, telling him he had to gain Kaas' trust and confidence. He was supposed to become Kaas' friend. When Keenan had asked for a clarification, the colonel had told him that Kaas' mother had been roughed up during a break-in, and he wanted Keenan to break the news to the corporal, let him call home on their sat phone, and offer any assistance.

The "home invasion" seemed pretty coincidental, and Keenan asked the colonel if he'd had anything to do with it.

"Goddamn it, Major! I've told you before that we are not the fucking CIA. We don't beat up women to get our way. But since it did happen, there's no use wasting the opportunity," the colonel had thundered over the phone.

"What if he wants emergency leave?" Keenan asked, not sure how to directly respond to the colonel's outburst.

"Sympathize, say you'll work on it and make him think you are, but it won't be approved. I can promise you that. You've disappointed me so far, Major, and it's about time you manned up. Get on his good side, but employ the bug. We need visual proof. Tarniton, out."

Keenan turned off the speaker, then looked up at MT, who'd been listening in.

"You got that thing?" Keenan asked.

MT held up a small, nondescript package that had come with the last helo lift into the FOB.

"And you know how to work it?"

MT nodded.

"Well, then, I guess we've got our marching orders. Let's see if he's available now. It's morning in Vegas, so the timing's right."

MT took a moment to prepare the small bug. This was getting to be too much for Keenan. The colonel was right. They weren't the CIA. They were the US Army, and this spy shit was getting pretty deep. Now he was the one to break the news to Kaas? What about the normal procedures, going through the Marine's chain of command? Wasn't it frigging weird that an outside Army major would take over this task? He should not be reaching out to a man in another command, and then keeping that contact secret as per the colonel's orders.

He was sure that the colonel had arranged for Kaas' mother's assault. And when MT stated his opinion, that pretty much cemented it for him. The question was what he would do about it. He was in the middle of the Hindu Kush, a long, long way from the Pentagon. He had to either march on or request a relief, and frankly, he had to admit to himself that he was a little concerned as to what would happen if he did that. COL Tarniton didn't seem to be a man who took refusal well.

Neither Keenan nor MT seemed to want to catch each other's eyes as they waited. Keenan almost wanted MT to suggest that they disobey orders. That would at least give him moral support. But

Army training was pretty strong, and disobeying a senior officer had to have a very strong and valid reason behind it.

After ten minutes of silence, there was a knock on the door.

"Enter!" Keenan barked out, a little more forcibly than he'd intended.

Aiden Kaas, a puzzled look on his face, entered and centered himself in the small space in front of Keenan's desk, came to attention, and said, "Corporal Kaas, reporting as ordered, sir!"

"Thank you for coming. Here, take off your battle rattle, son. You can hang it on the tree there," Keenan told him, pointing at the pieces of two-by-four that had been nailed together to make a short, upright T.

Most offices had the makeshift stands onto which body armor and webbing could be hung, close enough to don quickly if need be. Aiden looked over at the tree by the door, then almost warily took off his gear.

"Here, sit," Keenan continued as MT unfolded a small chair and placed it in front of the Marine.

Warily, almost as if he were a wild animal, Kaas carefully sat on the chair, his body posture a clear sign that he was nervous.

Is that because of my rank, or does he really have something to hide? Keenan wondered.

He'd had half an hour to prepare, but still, Keenan was not sure how to start. He looked at the ceiling of his plywood shack, marshalling his thoughts.

"Sir, I've got a girlfriend!" Kaas suddenly blurted out.

That was unexpected, to say the least. Keenan stared at the young man in confusion.

"What?" was about all he could muster.

"I've got a girlfriend, in Hawaii. We're gonna get married, too!"

"Well, uh, I thank you for sharing that. I'm not sure why you did, but—"

"Begging the major's pardon and all, and I'm not judging anyone, but I like girls!"

"WHAT?" Keenan yelled out, standing up as MT broke into uncontrolled laughter.

A panicked look crossed Kaas' face as he stammered out, "I mean —"

"I know what you mean, corporal, but where in hell's name did you get that idea!"

"I . . . I mean . . . the other guys, they said . . . oh, shit!" Kaas said, a look of mortification washing over his face.

Keenan glared at MT who was trying manfully to control his laughter.

I hope you choke, he thought, looking daggers at him.

He sat back down, and calmed himself. "You shouldn't pay attention to bullshit, corporal. I assure you, that there is nothing further from the truth."

"I'm sorry. I didn't mean to upset the major. I just thought . . . never mind that, sir. But why did you want to see me?" he asked.

That sobered the two soldiers up. No one liked to be the bearer of bad tidings.

"As the senior officer aboard the FOB, I have to give you some bad news," he began hoping that Kaas wouldn't realize that senior officer or not, as Kaas was not in his chain of command, it wasn't up to him to give Kaas the news. "Something happened to your mother."

"What happened?" Kaas asked, jumping up to stand over Keenan's desk. "Tell me!"

"Easy, son! She's OK, a little banged up, but OK. The police have responded, and I pulled in a few personal favors to get the Air Force MPs at Nellis on the scene and take care of her."

He went on to tell him the scenario, that it was a home invasion gone wrong, that his mother was roughed up. The two perpetrators ran off before they could steal anything, though.

As expected, Kaas immediately wanted to go home on emergency leave. "I've got to get there. There's nobody there to help her, and she doesn't have health insurance. She needs me!" he told Keenan.

As the colonel had ordered, Keenan promised to push through the request, knowing that was a flat-out lie. He hadn't thought about medical care, though, so he made a promise that he would ensure she was checked out by one of the doctors at the Nellis clinic.

That was against just about every regulation known to the military, but this promise, Keenan vowed he'd keep if he had to get the colonel to bring it up with the Chairman of the Joint Chiefs himself.

"Look, I've got my own sat phone here. It is for official business only, but I'd say this is official, wouldn't you agree, Specialist Sutikal?"

"Yes, sir, major. I'd say it is," MT answered.

"Here, take this phone. Why don't you step outside and call your mom. I'll get the ball rolling on getting her checked out, OK?"

A grateful Kaas took the phone and stepped out the door. Immediately, MT sprang into action. He carefully removed the tiny spy cam from its case and attached it inside one of the loops on the flak jacket, making a tiny hole in the material so the cam could view and record the scene. This was a very high piece of tech. It would not only record, but it would download the recording to a hard drive whenever the two pieces of equipment were within a klick or so of each other. With a quick application of extra material, the bug was almost unnoticeable. Keenan listened through the door to Kaas on the phone to make sure they weren't caught. Both men sat down with relief when the installation was complete.

A few minutes later, Kaas came back in the office and handed Keenan back the phone.

"How is she?" Keenan asked.

"Shaken up and bruised, but not hurt too bad," a somber Kaas answered. "I told her I was going to come home, but she said no, it wasn't necessary. She'd had worse from my father when he was still around, she said."

That made Keenan wince. These were real people, with real histories, and if the colonel was just treating them as pawns in some big game, then Keenan wanted no part in that.

"She refused treatment by the paramedics, but I told her you promised to send someone over to check her out. I really appreciate that, too, sir."

"Well, we have to look out after each other, right? I know it'll be hard, but why not go back and try to get some sleep? I'll let you know anything new that comes out of all of this. And if you need anything, *anything*, just let one of us know."

"Uh, well, OK. I'll let my lieutenant know I'm putting in for emergency leave. Thanks for all the major's help, sir. I really appreciate it."

Kaas came to attention, did a smart about face, then left the office.

"Check it out, MT," Keenan ordered.

MT pulled out the receiver and turned it on. The screen flickered, then the video appeared. It was jerking as Kaas walked, but it worked. At Keenan's nod, MT turned it off. The camera itself would be good for up to five days. After that, they'd have to retrieve it and change the battery, but that was another day's problem.

The two soldiers sat quietly for almost a minute before MT said in an affected voice, "But sir, I have a girlfriend!"

It was amazing how nimble a one-legged man could be while simultaneously laughing and dodging the manual Keenan threw at him.

Chapter 13

"You sure you don't want me to carry anything for you?" Aiden asked Hozan.

"No need. We are their guests, and they will provide," Hozan said, shrugging as Aiden stuffed his clothes into his assault pack.

Hozan had told Aiden they had been requested to visit Leewekhel again. Aiden had initially refused. If he wasn't out on a mission, his duty was to stay in the FOB. And what if someone came looking for him? He was still waiting for his emergency leave to get approved, and if that approval came in overnight, they'd be looking for him.

But Aiden was curious about the small tribe. Other than Hozan, he'd never met another werewolf who wasn't out to either kill or beat him senseless. Something about this tribe called to him. Hozan thought it was just Zakia's lingering "alphaness," but Aiden wasn't sure. Werewolves were now his "people," so to speak, and he wanted to know more about them, and by inference, about himself as well.

He didn't even try to justify the visit with a military reason. Sure, they might give him some worthwhile intel, if he asked, but that wasn't the reason he was going. He was going because he wanted to, nothing more.

Two of his team, Seth and Rob, tended to snore, and he had used that as an excuse to get out of his cot and find a quieter place to sleep. Others had done it before, so he doubted anyone would question that. If anyone did try to find him with his leave authorization, he'd just say he was racked out in one of the team's GMVs.

"Ready?" Aiden asked Hozan.

His friend didn't say anything. He just shifted, something that still freaked Aiden out to watch even after he'd done it himself so many times. It still helped Aiden to close his eyes to shift, but with

Hozan watching, he kept them open, triggering the transmogrification into his varg form.

As the night air became alive, Aiden struggled to get on his assault pack. His shoulders were not as flexible as when in human form, and he'd forgotten to extend the straps. With Hozan patiently waiting, he slipped the pack on and picked up his M4. Hozan had told him he didn't need it, but aside from simply feeling more secure with it, he couldn't very well just leave in lying out on the ground. He couldn't fit the flak jacket in his pack, so he had stashed it under an empty fuel drum, but if someone found the flak jacket while they were gone, no big whoop. A weapon, though, would be a different thing.

Hozan turned and with a huge leap, bounded up on top of the HESCO[35] barrier and disappeared over the edge. Aiden waited a moment to see if there was an outcry, and when things remained quiet, he followed. It still struck him as rather odd that someone as big as he was could move about so quietly and without causing a major commotion. He jumped down lightly on the other side, his huge thighs absorbing the impact. Hozan had already taken off, but with his varg nose, his friend might as well have left a string of chemlights. Aiden broke into a trot, and within a few moments, was out of the village adjacent to the FOB and into the forest.

He caught up to Hozan, and the two picked up their pace. Aiden had told Hozan that he had to be back by 0430—at the latest. By cutting off the path and climbing over some high areas, Hozan said they could be there in less than 90 minutes. With 90 minutes returning, that still would give them about two hours with the tribe. Whatever Zakia wanted, Aiden hoped they could get it done within that amount of time.

Aiden was breathing heavily as they climbed at a dead run, his lungs heaving like bellows. But it wasn't painful or particularly taxing to him. As a human, he would never have been able to keep up the pace, no matter how fit he was. It was at times like these that he marveled at what he had become and at the sheer power he now possessed.

---

[35] HESCO: an easily deployed barrier system that is filled with earth.

As they crested a small ridge, they surprised three *markhor*, a local deer, which bolted in a panic. Aiden almost took after them in pursuit, his hunting instincts taking over. Only Hozan's steady presence kept him grounded. He tested the breeze wistfully as he ran after his friend until he could no longer smell the animals.

Eventually, Aiden could pick out the scent of other werewolves. He was not sure if he was relieved or disappointed that he couldn't sense Zakia in her lycan form.

The two slowed to a trot and entered the small open area in the village. Except for a few small children who were in human form, everyone else was a varg, and they gathered around their two visitors, most of them obviously excited at the prospect of having guests. Aiden half expected them to all to sniff each other's butts.

How do we greet each other? Aiden wondered. He'd never thought to ask if there was any kind of secret handshake or whatever.

Aiden wasn't sure if he was supposed to shift back into human, but with everyone else a varg, he decided he'd wait until Hozan shifted.

As a varg, Aiden never sat down much. He could sort of settle on his haunches, but he didn't use chairs or such. It wasn't surprising to him then, that no one in the village sat. They moved en masse to the back of the village where a wicker dome held a number of chickens captive. One of the vargs reached under the dome and pulled out a squawking chicken. He ignored the wings flapping furiously as he brought the bird to Zakia. She took it, and with one quick bite, severed the head. She then offered the carcass to Hozan, who took it and bit off a chunk of the trembling body before handing it back to the alpha. She then turned to Aiden and offered him the dripping bird.

The thought of raw, bloody meat still bothered him in the recesses of his human mind, but in the here and now, as a varg, he started salivating. Part of him wanted to turn away, but he took the chicken, and seeing how much Hozan had bitten, took an equal amount in one bite. He handed the remains back to Zakia as the hot blood coursed down his throat, the coppery flavor sending almost electric jolts of pleasure through him. Hozan had warned him a multitude of times about the dangers of going feral, and it was in times like this that he had to acknowledge the attraction to just shucking the world of man away and running wild in the mountains. He wanted to go back and find those *markhor* and run them down.

More chickens were brought out, and each member of the tribe took a bite, even the small children still in human form, the blood running down their chubby cheeks. Aiden realized that this was a ritual of sorts, but he didn't know if it was an Afghan thing or a werewolf thing.

After the last chicken had been consumed, a few of the tribe shifted back into human form, some to take care of the children, some to take a seat and sip shomleh. Most remained in varg form, though, and as Hozan hadn't shifted, neither did Aiden. He stood there, just taking in the scene while Zakia, Hozan, and another male talked. Aiden's ears were more than good enough to hear what they were saying, but as he didn't speak Farsi, he just ignored them.

One female walked right up to him and spoke in guttural Pashto.

"Za na poheegum," he said, his stock Pashto phrase.

She seemed to find that funny, as did others around them, all leaning back and making the stuttered howl that Aiden knew was varg laughter.

Aiden knew she was interested in him in a physical way, even though he wasn't sure how. But he was certain of that. Maybe it was those pheromones Hozan had told him about. She wasn't in lycan form, but still, something was going on there.

Aiden was still getting used to his varg body, and years of human imprinting had cemented into his mind what was a good looking woman. A big, hairy varg didn't fit the bill, but still, something piqued his curiosity. He wondered what she would look like as a human, and he was tempted to shift back to see if she would follow. He was also well aware that they would both be naked if they shifted.

Thoughts of Claire flitted in the back of his mind like a butterfly trying to get out of a net. He tried to ignore them. He loved Claire, and no mountain varg was going to replace her, but still, his body was responding, and he couldn't help but wonder what or even how two vargs got it on. Around her were at least six or seven other vargs, and he didn't get a feeling that any of the males were taking offense at her interest. Once again, he wondered at how much Pashtun Afghan and how much werewolf these people were. He didn't think the overt physical interest would be aimed at him in another Afghan village.

The rest of the evening was spent with the vargs teaching him various words in Pashto. With the varg vocal chords constraining what he could say, the others seemed to take delight in his pronunciation. At one point, they brought forward a little boy, no more than four years old, and had the boy, with his clearer human pronunciation, speak words for him to repeat.

With a little human boy surrounded by towering werewolves, this wasn't a Norman Rockwell painting, but still, it somehow had a down-home feel to it. And that made Aiden happy. He felt like he finally belonged somewhere, or at least had found someplace where he *could* belong if he so chose.

He was disappointed when Hozan broke off his talks with Zakia and the other elders. It was time to leave. He picked up his small teacher and held the boy high, saying "*da khoday pa amaan,*" which he was sure meant "goodbye. The boy's giggling human laughter was a counterpoint to the howling laughter of the vargs, and Aiden let loose, turning his laughter into a long, drawn-out howl.

He didn't want to leave, and he wondered what would happen if he stayed. It wasn't a serious thought, though. He was a Marine, and he had his team back at the FOB. Then there was Claire and his mom. No, he was not going to stay, but the thought has some allure.

He and Hozan took their leave of the village, but before they started to run, Aiden stopped Hozan and asked what the purpose of the visit was.

"First, they decided that they had to know what was going on in the world of man. They wanted to know who was in their mountains, who was fighting who. They have been isolated for a very long time, and Zakia felt she had to understand the situation in order to better protect her people."

"That's it? But why did I have to come?"

"Because you are one of the foreigners, and they wanted to take a measure, as you say it, right? To take a measure of what your people are. And they wanted to see if you would fit in, in case they need new blood in their tribe. Even they know the dangers of inbreeding."

"New blood? Inbreeding? They want babies?" Aiden asked, shocked.

"Isn't that the natural condition? To have healthy young to carry on to the future?"

"Yeah, but, I don't . . . I mean, we're not . . . I can't even communicate with them. How can I do them any good? Even if I wanted to, that is."

"It seems to me you were communicating pretty well with Kashmala, there."

"That girl? We never understood a single word from each other," Aiden protested.

As Hozan broke out into a trot, he turned back and said, "You don't need speaking for what she might want, now, do you? There are other ways to communicate."

He thinks this is fucking funny! Aiden thought as he broke out into a run after him. *It's patently ridiculous, isn't it?*

Still, imagined images that both intrigued and scared him at the same time kept popping into his mind as he ran back with Hozan to the FOB.

Chapter 14

Keenan stared at the frozen frame on the screen, trying to will it to come into better focus. He just couldn't tell.

"I don't know," MT said, looking over his shoulder.

One thing for sure was that Cpl Kaas had done something out of the ordinary last night, but what, neither of them knew. It could have been sneaking off to get laid, assuming prostitution even existed in the decrepit village outside the FOB. More likely, there was some black marketeering going on. In that case, Kaas was a criminal and should be court-martialed.

What neither of them expected was that before doing whatever he was going to do, he took off his battle rattle and dumped the gear behind some of the empty wooden crates in back of the motor pool. The camera caught a glimpse of another person, whom Keenan would have to track down, then the flak jacket was dropped behind the crates, giving the spycam only a tiny field of vision. It was what they saw, or maybe didn't see, that was giving them pause. The spycam was top of the line, but the lens was tiny, so both the quality and light-gathering capability were limited. So when something barely grazed the field of view, neither one of them could swear as to what it was. Given that the cam was pointed at the dirt, it was a good bet that the image was the edge of a foot. But what they couldn't confirm was if that foot was in a boot or not. Very little of it flashed in front of the cam's field of view, and it was moving fast, but something seemed off. Keenan just couldn't see enough to say just what. Was it really possible that Aiden was an honest to goodness werewolf? Was the colonel right about all of this? Or were the two of them seeing things that just weren't there?

Keenan's contact within the team hadn't seen anything yet. The spycam recording showed nothing. The whole concept of real werewolves was pretty difficult to accept, and the colonel notwithstanding, neither he nor MT was convinced. Yet something was weird about the corporal. That alone was proof of nothing, however. They had to have solid evidence to prove it, but if he was just a tough son of a bitch with no paranormal abilities, how do you go about proving that? How do you prove a negative?

"There isn't enough here," Keenan said at last. "I'm not going to send this up and have the colonel all over our asses when this could be, probably is, nothing."

The colonel had been ramping up the pressure, but Keenan thought that a false-positive would be much worse than no indication at all. The most logical course of action would be to wait until they had something stronger, one way or the other.

Chapter 15

"I can't believe it. You knew her?" Aiden asked Manny.

"Well, like I said, bro, I knew *of* her. It wasn't like we were close. 'Sides, back then, little guys didn't like the little girls."

"I heard you still didn't like girls, Manny," Cree said, but without conviction from his cot where he was reading a graphic novel.

When a team member left himself open to a barb like that, it had to be exploited.

"Fuck you, too," Manny said in an equally rote manner.

"I mean, we were in grade school, so it was a long time ago," Manny continued to Aiden.

"Was she a bitch then, too?" Aiden asked.

"Certifiably, bro, certifiably."

Aiden hadn't even known Manny was a Vegas native until this afternoon. His family moved to Bakersfield before junior high, and neither of them had crossed paths until joining the team. Now, in one of those million-to-one shots, it turned out that Manny knew Teri Brubaker, the girl whose rejection had spurred Aiden to enlist.

Aiden had heard Manny mention John Mull's Meats and Roadkill Grill, a longtime local Vegas BBQ joint, and that opened up the entire conversation that gravitated to whom they knew in common. Aiden gleefully related the misfortune that had befallen on Teri and her then-boyfriend Ben Souter since high school.

Aiden had come to like the JTAC. Manny had not been through any of the recon pipeline, and as neither Aiden nor Doc had done the A&S, that gave them a commonality. Manny was a good Marine, though, which was not surprising as not many Marines were given the opportunity to become JTACs. They had to be shit-hot when controlling the awesome capability of the Coalition air power. A tiny slipup and civilians or Marines could be blown away.

Aiden and Doc went back further, but along with Cree and Brett, Manny was probably his closest friend. The entire team was tight, and Aiden had no issues with anyone, but he seemed to spend most of his free time shooting the shit, working out, or playing cards with those four men.

Chapter 16

Over the next ten days, Aiden twice went with Hozan up to the village. Aiden chose to ignore the fact that when Hozan had first arrived, he warned Aiden about shifting at all, and now he was encouraging it. Hozan told him it was good for him to be around other vargs, to socialize and begin to understand what it was like to be in a tribe.

The fact that Hozan himself did not live in a tribe was not lost on Aiden, but the one time that Aiden had asked about it, Hozan had abruptly and firmly cut him off. Aiden knew Hozan had had a family, and something had happened to them before the war, but that was about it. Aiden could see that Hozan relaxed more with the vargs of the village. The little trips might be good for Aiden, but they were also good for Hozan, Aiden realized. They were helping his friend heal.

Aiden had hoped to see Zakia as a lycan again. The thought excited him in ways he didn't quite understand. Part of it felt like titillation, but it was more of a need to bask in her presence. She never shifted all the way, though. She was either human or varg, and that was it.

Hozan explained that shifting to lycan took a lot out of them and that too much time as a lycan could take years off of a life. It also increased the chances of going feral, and the tribe could not afford that. If the Council knew of this small tribe, it would already consider it feral and fair game for elimination. There were occasionally small tribes like this one that were known by some, but as long as they kept out of sight, they were allowed to exist. But if they drew attention to themselves and became an issue for the Tribe as a whole, then the more reactionary members of the Council would insist on extermination.

Aiden couldn't imagine this happy, peaceful tribe suffering that fate. He had almost begun to think of them as his tribe, as his family. That bothered him, to an extent. His mother back in Las

Vegas was his family. He'd grown up human, after all. He loved Claire and wanted to marry her. Still, he didn't know how else to describe his feelings. The tribe *felt* like family.

Kashmala's obvious interest in him also made him feel uncomfortable, but deep inside, he enjoyed her almost possessive claim on him. She was always with him when he was there. Neither one of them could communicate well without the help of others, but he was surprised at how quickly he was picking up Pashto. Kashmala seemed to take great pleasure in honchoing his learning.

If there was a little lust in his feelings for her, he tried to suppress that. He loved Claire, simple as that. But still, he couldn't ignore what his body was telling him, and he was sure Kashmala would be receptive to anything he suggested. He felt like he was flirting with danger, and that excited him in its own right. She was not Claire, but there was an underlying attraction there. Maybe Hozan had been right about those pheromone things.

Chapter 17

Nikolai Borisov took a moment to look into the screen before asking, "So, there is no objection if I take action?"

He was not used to video conferencing, but it saved him a trip back to Germany, and he didn't have to wait for others on the Council to arrive if a quorum was not already there. This new technology was certainly convenient, but without the others there in the room with him, he couldn't use his nose to gauge the others.

Nikolai was on the Council, but he wasn't exactly a very active member. He'd gotten his position due to the prominence of his family in the Tribe, nothing more. The Council wisely sought representation from all the major families, but many of those families only gave lip service to the concept of an overarching Council, the Borisovs among them. Nikolai was happy to remain in Uzbekistan with his reach into Afghanistan, Pakistan, and Tajikistan and run his family business. He had placed members of his family into influential positions in the human governments, and this gave him practical immunity to carry on his activities.

The entry of the American-led Coalition forces into Afghanistan and the pressure they put on the Pakistani government had an impact on some of his more lucrative enterprises, but for the most part, it was business as usual, just as it had been for decades. The Soviets had not been an impediment, and neither would the Americans be one. The Taliban were nothing, either. Although they professed their loathing for many of the types of business that Nikolai controlled, in actuality, they were ready and willing allies when it came down to it.

Frankly, Nikolai didn't care if the Taliban and the Coalition forces killed each other off, as long as they left him alone. Business was business, and nothing could interfere with that. And that was why he had requested the Council meeting. Something had interfered, and as much as he tried to ignore the Council, taking action against the feral tribe that had attacked his shipment required Council approval. He risked more than he wanted to if he took unilateral action against another tribe, even a feral one.

Nikolai was well aware that most of the others on the Council looked down on him. They did not approve of his various enterprises. Several times, they had tried to get him to back off, afraid that he would attract unwanted attention to the Tribe. The drugs and weapons smuggling were bad enough, but putting tribe members into the human government seemed pure idiocy to them. But when two of his most vocal opponents simply disappeared, the rest backed down.

Sheep, he thought as he waited for a reply. *All sheep, afraid to take what is rightfully ours!*

"Unless anyone objects, I have to agree with Counsel Borisov. We cannot have a feral tribe attacking any of us," Günter Wais said.

Nikolai had no allies on the Council, but Wais was as close to one as he had. Wais shared some of Nikolai's philosophy on the position of the Tribe with regards to the humans. Nikolai had supported Wais several times when he'd bothered to get involved with Tribal politics, so he wasn't surprised that Wais would support him on this. Nikolai knew that Wais would expect a return favor, but that didn't bother him. He'd support Wais or not based on the situation at the time.

"I have no objection," Park Ho Mun said. "However, any action Counsel Borisov takes against the ferals must be made with Tribe only, no humans. We cannot allow humans to take part in any action against us."

There were nods of agreement from the other Council members.

Piss on you, Nikolai thought.

The Borisov tribe was old and fairly large, but he didn't have enough of them who would be willing to attack another tribe, even a feral one who had attacked one of his operations. He needed about 100 fighting vargs to be sure to overcome the 80 or so ferals, of which probably 20-30 were prime fighters. Nikolai had intended to use some of his human vassals to bolster his numbers. He wasn't so out of touch that he'd have allowed any of them to live after the attack. No human who had shed Tribe blood, even feral blood, could be allowed that, after all. Now, with this stricture, he'd have to raise 30-40 vargs from outside his tribe, and that would indebt him to those Alphas. Nikolai felt no compulsion to repay Wais for his support, but within the central Asian region, these personal debts could not so easily be ignored.

"Of course, Counsel Park," Nikolai said, trying to sound as if that had been his plan all along.

There were a few more comments, but Nikolai knew he'd get the Council's approval. The feral tribe was out of the Council's control, so giving Nikolai the go-ahead to eliminate the tribe made it his headache instead of theirs. It was a foregone conclusion, but Nikolai knew he had to play the game and formally request permission.

There was not a single voice of dissent. Nikolai had his permission. He'd already had his assault force ready for the attack, but because of that cub-faced Park, he would have to delay it and find additional vargs to join his team.

No matter. Tomorrow or a week from now, that feral tribe in the Hindu Kush would be no more.

Chapter 18

"He leaves at night sometimes, coming back in before dawn," HM2 Redmond said, standing in front of Keenan. "I don't think I've ever seen him leave, though. I just look up, and he's not in his rack."

Keenan looked up at the corpsman. The doc didn't seem comfortable even relaying that small piece of information, and Keenan didn't feel right forcing it from him. Due to his untimely accident in Kuwait, Keenan had never seen combat, but he knew that teamwork and trust were vital to a unit's combat effectiveness. Turning the doc into a spy couldn't be good for the team, and that could have unforeseen consequences. But the colonel had given him the information on Redmond that ensured his cooperation. Keenan had spoken to the corpsman before he'd been assigned to MSOC, letting him know that the young man had a good career ahead of him, and it would be a shame if some youthful extravagances, as he put it, would get in the way of that career. If he would only keep an eye on Kaas and report back anything unusual, well, he would make sure that all records of an "unsavory nature" would be destroyed, and Redmond would be in the clear. Keenan didn't have to get into the details: Redmond understood and agreed to watch Kaas.

Keenan had felt dirty then, and he felt dirty now. He resented the shit out of the colonel for putting him in this position. He was really beginning to resent the shit out of the entire operation. Whatever Kaas was or wasn't, he wanted to tell the colonel to shove it, and if that was the end of his career, if you could even call it that, then so be it.

"That's it? Nothing else?" he asked the corpsman.

"Yes, sir, that's it," Redmond said.

Keenan stared at the young man's face, wondering if the corpsman was holding anything back. Marines tended to cover each other's ass, and while Navy, Redmond was, for all intents and purposes, a Marine as far as his team went.

"Very well. Just keep an eye on him," he said, ignoring his suspicion. Then, he added, "You are doing well. Corporal Kaas is important to our mission for reasons I can't say right now, and we've got to make sure he's around to do his job. We've got to have his back."

He had taken this tack earlier, figuring he'd get better cooperation if the doc thought he was watching out for Kaas instead of doing something that might hurt the Marine. Something told him, though, that Redmond was not buying it. Keenan could see it in his eyes.

"If that's all, then you're dismissed. Specialist Sutikal will let you know next time I need a report."

HM2 Redmond came to attention, did an about-face, and not saluting as was the norm for Marines and sailors when indoors, left the room. Keenan looked over at MT as the door closed.

"Well?" he asked his assistant.

"I don't think we'd get anything from him if he saw anything," MT responded. "He sure as hell didn't want to be here today."

"I think you're right there. But we had to get this report before calling the colonel. And speaking of which, I guess I can't put that off any longer."

Keenan took out the sat phone and punched in the colonel's number. It would be almost 0700 at the Pentagon, but Keenan knew Colonel Tarniton would be in. Sure enough, after only one ring, the colonel came on the phone.

"Well?" he asked without a preamble.

"Sir, we've still got nothing solid. We just debriefed HM2 Redmond, and he had nothing to add."

"And the cam, that's shown nothing?"

"No, sir, nothing," Keenan said, glancing up at MT who stared back at him with deadpan eyes.

"Well shit. And that corpsman? He's seen nothing at all?"

"That's what he says, sir."

"And do you believe him?"

Keenan didn't really believe the corpsman 100%, but he was not going to tell the colonel that.

"Yes, sir. I do," Keenan answered.

"Well you're a fool, Major. These people, they'll hide anything to protect one of their own. You've got to be more forceful in getting it out of him. Maybe I'll leak some of that pervert's secrets out and see if that'll get him to be more forthcoming."

"Sir?" Keenan asked, shocked.

"You've got a problem with that, Major?" the colonel's voice came cold and hard over the phone.

"Well, well, yes, sir, I do. I told him on my honor that if he cooperated with us, all of that would be destroyed," Keenan said, his vehemence surprising him and drawing a raised eyebrow from MT.

"I don't give a fuck for your honor, Major. You West Pointers live and die by your vaunted Honor Code, but in the real world, it isn't that simple. What we are doing is for the United States, and if we have to sacrifice a piddly-ass Navy corpsman for that—and your precious honor—then I have no hesitation in my heart but to do it. Do you understand me?"

"Uh, yes, sir," Keenan said outwardly while his conscience silently screamed out "*No!*"

"Good. I'm glad we're on the same page. And your charm offensive on Kaas, has he seemed to open up to you yet?"

"It's hard to say—" Keenan began before the colonel cut him off.

"It's hard to fucking say? What is your malfunction, Major? I hired you because some people thought you had what it takes despite being a cripple. I took you because I thought you could get the job done. And now you tell me 'It's hard to say?'"

"No, sir. I can say. We've had conversations, and he seems to trust me. But he hasn't come out and told me he's a fucking werewolf!" Keenan said with more force than he was used to when speaking to a senior officer.

If the colonel noticed the lack of deference, or even cared, he didn't show it. "I thought that it might work. Guess I was wrong. We wasted an operation on the kid's mother, and I don't think we can do that again. So we need to go further. I've got a few ideas, so Major, you and your specialist, I want you two to get into Kaas' head. Make him think you're his friends, part of his team. I'll be back to you with further instructions in a day or so as I work some things out. Tarniton, out."

Keenan pulled down the phone so he could stare into the receiver in shock. The colonel has just "wasted an operation" having to do with Kaas' mother? That asshole had arranged for the break-in and assault and had lied to Keenan about it. What the hell had he gotten himself into? He was taking orders from a man who ordered a civilian woman roughed up? This was not what he'd signed up for.

He looked up at MT who merely shrugged back at him. Keenan didn't think that his assistant caught the significance of the colonel's words, and until he wrapped his own head around them, Keenan wasn't sure he should point that out.

Keenan didn't know what he should do. He couldn't very well report what the colonel was doing, given the security clearance on this operation, and even if he wanted to, he had no idea to whom he would report. As far as he knew, his chain of command went up to the colonel, and then from him to someone very high on the pecking order. The only thing Keenan was sure of was that he'd just about had it. If what their little command was doing wasn't illegal, it was morally reprehensible.

With that realization, Keenan reached a decision. There was one thing he could do, should do, and the colonel had pretty much ordered him to do it.

"MT, why don't you see if you can round up the good corporal," he told his assistant. "The team's going out tonight, and I want to talk to him before that."

"Roger that. Let me go track him down," MT responded, getting up from his chair and leaving the office.

Keenan leaned back in his chair as far as the cramped space would let him, clasping his hands in back of his neck as he stared at the plywood ceiling. Kaas' team would be rotating back to the US before too long, and once that was done, Keenan would be out of this Godforsaken FOB where he had no real purpose. He outranked everyone else in the FOB, yet he and MT were superfluous bodies, suspected of being spies for higher headquarters. Captain Lindon certainly suspected that, and he wasn't very circumspect about it when the two spoke. The ironic thing was that while the captain was right, Keenan wasn't spying on him. The captain was safe in his little fiefdom.

It took almost 30 minutes before MT returned with Kaas. The Marine corporal looked slightly exasperated at having to come see him, but he was obviously trying to control that. Keenan looked at his watch. It was almost chow time, he realized, and one of the things that HM2 Redmond had said was that Kaas never missed chow when he could help it and ate more than anyone else on the team.

"Specialist Sutikal, would you give us a few minutes?"

MT looked surprised and seemed almost to say something, but he nodded and left the office. Keenan gestured at MT's seat, and Kaas hesitantly took it.

Make friendly with Kaas, he wanted? OK, he ordered it.

"I'm sorry to pull you now. I know you're going out in a couple of hours. I wanted to come clean with you. Do you know why I've had an interest in you?" he asked.

"Uh, no, not really sir," Kaas said cautiously.

"There is something different about you, something special, something unique."

Keenan was rewarded with a jerk of the head and a look of guilt. Whatever skills or capabilities Kaas had, lying wasn't one of them. That in itself was not damning, but the analytical part of Keenan's mind took note of the corporal's reaction.

"Now, I'm not asking you to tell me just what you can do, even though some people, and I mean people high up, have some suspicions, and they sent me here to confirm just what it is about you that is different. If you want to tell me, fine, I am here to listen. But it's up to you."

Keenan stared pointedly at the corporal, but the young man had seemingly regained his composure and said nothing.

"But I want to tell you that someone, and I can't say who, is after your ass. He wants your secrets. And, I am sorry to say, the whole thing with your mother was a sham, designed to seek my help."

Keenan held up his hand to stop the corporal who had jumped up out of his seat.

"Your mother was never in any danger," he said, silently hoping that was the truth. "Some idiot thought it would spark you into revealing yourself. I knew nothing about it until just now. Please, sit."

Kaas didn't look mollified, but he did sink back into MT's chair. He hadn't jumped over Keenan's desk to attack him, and given the corporal's combat record, Keenan thought that in itself was a victory for him.

"I wanted to be blunt with you. Your mother wasn't in danger, as I just found out, but someone wants your secrets. You need to watch yourself. I am supposed to be watching you, and I don't know why, but from what I can observe, I see before me a warrior, a patriot. I think you are fighting for the US and are a good Marine, so I see no reason not to level with you."

Kaas still said nothing but stared at him, and Keenan couldn't read what was going one behind those deep hazel eyes.

"I'm going to let you go, but one thing. If you need anything, *anything*, you let me know. I may only be a major, but I've got a lot of pull. I'm here for you, so don't hesitate to use me.

"Do you have any questions? Anything you want to say?"

"No, sir. I don't know what you're talking about, but I'm going to trust you that my mom's OK. I think it's crazy shit that anyone is taking an interest in me, but I thank you for telling me that. Can I go now?"

The kid was covering up something, and despite Keenan's less-than-convinced belief in werewolves, he couldn't help but feel a twinge of excitement.

"Yeah, sure. I know you need to finish getting ready. Be safe out there, and remember, I'm here if you need me."

Kaas stood up, came to attention, and after a hesitation, rendered a salute. Keenan stood to return it. Technically, on an Army installation, salutes were rendered indoors and when uncovered in situations like these, but Marines didn't salute indoors, and Kaas had never done that before. Keenan dared to hope that his talk might have sunk into the corporal.

MT came back in immediately after Kaas left.

"Well?" he asked.

"The colonel said get closer to Kaas, so that's just what I did," he replied.

Only, if Tarniton knew just how he'd accomplished that, the colonel would have his ass.

Chapter 19

Shit, shit shit!

Aiden rushed to the DFAC, his mind a jumble. If what the major had said was true, then someone knew what he was, and that couldn't be good. And whoever it was fucked with his mother? It had been difficult for Aiden to hold back from attacking the major when he'd said that. He probably would have before the major had said he just found out about it, but he'd been so pissed that he'd started to shift and had had to clamp down on that.

He believed the major, though, that he had not been in on it. Someone had, however, and Aiden made a solemn promise that he'd find out who and extract some justice. If they wanted him out in the open, whoever "they" were, they should confront him, not his mother!

He subconsciously shifted one finger to his varg claw, an exercise he'd been doing for some time now to hone his control. It was as if his claw was seeking the men who'd invaded his mother's home and threatened her.

Despite his agitation, or maybe because of it, he was starving, and he knew he had to fuel his body before going out on their planned five-day mission. He knew he needed more food after shifting, but could stress also require more calories?

He grabbed his chow and went to join the rest of the team, who were busily shoveling in the Salisbury steak main course or the ever-present burgers and dogs.

"What did your boyfriend want?" Cree asked before suggestively sliding his hot dog in and out of his mouth.

"He wanted to know why I hung out with such dicks and offered me a job as a contract killer at $300k per year," he responded before sitting down.

He'd been around long enough to dish it out stronger than it came in. Anything else was a sign of weakness and would only invite more shit.

Inside, though, he was worried sick. Just what did they know, and who knew it? It was bad enough that half of the Council wanted him dead, but if the US government, his own government, was after him, too, then he was up shit creek without a paddle. Major Ward seemed to be on his side, but that didn't mean those over him had Aiden in his best interests.

He kept looking around, and as expected, Hozan somehow felt Aiden's anxiety and came out of the galley, where he'd been working. He caught Aiden's eye, and Aiden nodded, their signal that he needed to talk to his friend. He had to tell Hozan what had happened. This was all too much for Aiden, and he couldn't handle it alone.

Chapter 20

It had been a quiet two weeks without any contact. The team had gone out continuously but had observed nothing out of the ordinary. The infantry company had been more aggressive in its patrolling, and they'd had no action, either. Despite this, Aiden was antsy as they sat high on a mountainside, eyes observing the pass below them. He didn't know why his nerves were crawling. He couldn't sense anything, nor had there been any reports of Taliban activity. But something had him on edge. The team had been in position since the night before, and Aiden had felt fine then. It was only sometime during the day that he'd started feeling anxious.

"Your friend up there see anything?" Aiden asked Manny.

The two Marines shared an outcropping of rock that gave them a good view of the pass below. Manny had out his MVR III, the small handheld video display from which he could see, in real time, what the orbiting A-10 Warthog had on its own systems. Whatever the pilot could see was relayed down to Manny's MVR III as well.

"Nothing since the last time you asked, what five minutes ago?" Manny told him. "What's up with you?"

"Nothing. I just feel something's not right out there. Call it my gut," Aiden told him.

"It's not like anyone can sneak up on us, Aiden," Manny said.

That was an understatement. The team was spread out over a small ledge that ran alongside the mountain. Below was a drop of almost 500 feet. Above them, the mountainside got steeper as it rose another 300 feet to the summit. No one was going to be assaulting them from below or above. They wouldn't be assaulting anyone themselves, either. This was strictly observation. An Army platoon was below them and a klick to the east, searching a tiny hamlet for a weapons cache that intel said was there. If the Taliban moved to strike at them, the team would see that and call in for air.

With an A-10 on station and a flight of B-1's on call, no one was getting through the pass without the team's approval.

This was an easy mission, a low-stress mission.

So why am I so freaked out about it?

He concentrated on calming himself. He couldn't function if he let the stress get to him. Despite Hollywood movies to the contrary, a hyped-up or angry soldier was a liability rather than an effective fighter.

"What the fuck is that?" Manny muttered.

"What?" Aiden asked as his nerves came alive.

"This," Manny said, swinging around his laptop so Aiden could see. "We've got some movement, but something's fucked up. Whatever's down there is moving pretty fast."

Aiden looked at the video screen to the image of where the orbiting A-10 had its FLIR[36] camera trained on some trees. Shapes moved on the screen, but it was hard to make them out. Manny was right, though. They were moving fast.

"Where is that?" Aiden asked, his foreboding getting stronger.

"Uh, about, let's see, about 200 meters from M22, moving east to west."

"M22" was one of the reference points Manny had on his map which made it easier to call for air support. In a village, the reference points were typically buildings easily identified from above. They were out in the mountains, though, so in this case, most of the reference points were unusual rock formations or mounting peaks.

Both Manny and Aiden automatically looked up and across the valley to the high ground on the other side. They were too far away to see anything, but as Aiden looked back to the screen, something seemed to click in his mind. He looked farther to the northwest, to where the varg village was just below the peak barely visible to their position.

"What are they? Deer? Do they have that many deer here?" Manny asked.

---

[36] FLIR: Forward Looking Infrared, a cameras system that uses the infrared spectrum to see a target.

Suddenly, he knew why he'd been uneasy. The shapes were not deer. They were vargs, and they were moving to the village. This was not a social call. The Council had decided to take action on what they considered a feral tribe. Aiden was positive about this.

"Manny, can you call air in on them?" Aiden asked.

"What the fuck? Call air on a herd of deer?"

"Those aren't deer. Those are Taliban, and they are going to double back and hit the platoon. We need to stop them now while they are on the plateau over there and before they get into the canyon walls.

"Shit, Aiden, are you crazy? How the hell do you know those are Taliban?"

"Look at them," Aiden said, grasping at anything that would make sense. "I saw an RPG right there on your screen. You didn't see it? And do those look like deer?"

The FLIR used infrared as a source and could show shapes, but seeing a specific weapon was problematic. The shapes, though, did look more like humans than quadrupedal deer.

"Nah, I don't see any weapons," Manny said. "And how do you know they are going to come back? I mean, look at their direction. They're going away from Charlie One down there."

"I . . . well . . . look, I can't tell you everything, but I am privy to some classified shit, and, uh, intel knows the Taliban are massing," he said, scrambling for a reason. "I kid you not, this is a no-shit HVT.[37]

"I don't know. Let me ask Norm," Manny said, not convinced.

Aiden beat him to it, raising Norm on the squad radio. "Norm, this is Aiden. We've got a large group of Taliban spotted on the FLIR. They are moving to attack Charlie One. We need to request an air strike, over."

There was a pause, then "Give me the details."

Aiden took the positions from the laptop, then confirmed a positive ID of armed Taliban. Manny started to key in when Aiden smacked his shoulder and held up his hand to stop many from transmitting that there was no positive ID.

---

[37] HVT: High Value Target

"From what you're telling me, they are moving away from Charlie One. What makes you think they are going to come back to attack, over?"

"You need to trust me on this, Norm. Please, over."

There was a long pause, then, "Call it in. Well let the CP decide, over."

Manny was shaking his head at Aiden. "Positive confirmation? What the fuck, Aiden?"

"Just send in your nine-line,[38] OK? I'll explain later. Warheads on their foreheads, that's what you keep saying, right?"

Manny looked at Aiden for a moment as if contemplating something else, but he sighed, then passed his nine-line. Then it was a waiting game. Air missions were not just made and executed by the ground JTAC and the pilot. The mission had to go back to the CP, where it would be vetted with the area commander or his rep. The ROEs in the theater were pretty stringent, and each mission had to get a command OK.

"What the hell?" Manny asked as they waited. "That was a fucking dog there. Since when did the Taliban start using dogs?"

That was a valid question. In the Muslim world, dogs were considered unclean animals, and the Taliban did not use them in the same way as western forces used combat dogs.

Aiden knew that the "dog" had to be a lycan, but he couldn't very well tell Manny that.

"They just probably scared up a fox or something. They're running pretty fast, after all, not trying to go stealth-mode."

Manny grunted, obviously not mollified. The A-10 continued to orbit, training its FLIR on the ground from 20,000 feet. Aiden hoped it would come lower where the resolution on its FLIR would be more precise.

Manny's radio finally came to life. He listened for a moment before giving a roger.

"No go on the air. The command says there is no proof they are Taliban and that they are going to attack Charlie One."

---

[38] Nine-line: slang for a call for supporting air. There are nine lines of information which are given to enable a successful strike.

"Fuck no! We've got to hit them!" Aiden exclaimed.

"Sorry, no go. Look, I love you like a brother, but this is some iffy shit. I sent in the nine-line, but that's all we can do. I'm going to tell Norm."

"No! Send it again!"

"Shit, Aiden! Why's this so important to you? They're just going to refuse it again. Hell, those could be friendlies, and you know what happened up in Bala Murghab when the air was called in on those SOF."

Aiden stared at the mass of images continuing west to the village. He had to do something, and he had his ace in the hole.

"Look, tell them to get Major Ward on the hook."

"That one-legged major? What the hell's going on here?"

"Just do it. Trust me. I'll fill you in later on what I can," Aiden said, leaving the last purposefully misleading.

If he could use the veil of classified information, he would.

Manny didn't want to place the call, and Aiden watched the emotions play across his face, but finally, he relented. Then it was another waiting game while the varg pack kept closing the distance to the village. They were less than four klicks now, the best Aiden could figure.

It was 12 minutes before the major made it to the CP and came on the line. Manny handed his headset to Aiden.

"Major, this is Corporal Kaas. Please listen. There is a Taliban force moving to attack Charlie One, and we need to act immediately to stop them. The CP has refused to authorize the strike, but that is a mistake, over."

"Uh, Corporal Kaas, I'm not sure what you want me to do. That's a command decision, over," the major passed.

"If the decision was made by the Charlie Six,[39] you can override that if you were up front with me, over."

"And why would I want to, corporal?" the major asked, his voice quieter as if he had stepped to the side so as not to be overheard.

---

[39] Charlie Six: "Six" refers to the commander. Charlie Six would be the Charlie Company commander.

"Major, you told me that some people thought there was something, uh, *different* about me. Well, there might be, and I'll brief you on what I can when I get back. Please trust me that the Taliban have to be hit, and I don't have time to go through proper channels. I need your help, and I need it now. You told me I can count on you for anything. Trust me, please, over."

Fuck! Where am I getting this bullshit? he wondered. *I'll worry about that later.*

There was silence as Aiden impatiently waited for a response. Finally, the radio keyed in.

"I'll see what I can do, but you and I are going to have another talk when you get back. Ward, out."

"You are either seriously connected, or you are in deep, deep shit, my friend," Manny said as Aiden handed him back his headset.

"Just don't say anything to the others, OK?" Aiden asked before lapsing into silence.

The two sat and waited for a decision. Manny was in comms with the pilot, who was getting low on fuel and would have to leave the station soon. The vargs were getting closer to the village, and soon it would be too late. Aiden had to restrain himself from shifting right then and there and rushing off.

Fifteen minutes later, Manny received the response. He looked at Aiden in surprise.

"The mission is approved," he said to Aiden's relief.

The pilot had received the same word, so Manny passed it up to Norm as the two Marines watched ten klicks away and across the valley.

"No way they're trying to attack Charlie One," Manny said.

Aiden ignored him.

A streak of fire, barely visible against the backdrop of the far mountain, plunged to the ground. The A-10's GAU-8/A Avenger 30mm automatic cannon rained 50 rounds within the first second before reaching its max of 70 rounds every second. Aiden tried to imagine the big armor-piercing depleted uranium rounds pulverizing the varg pack. Some seconds later, the roar of the gun reached the Marines. The Warthog made four runs before backing off

"What about the Mavericks?" Aiden asked, referring to the air-to-ground missiles the plane carried.

"Low on fuel," Manny told him. "But in for a penny. We've got a B-1 waiting to hit them. You had better be right about all of this is all I can say."

The B-1 would be orbiting at 30,000 feet or so. When the A-10 cleared the area, it started its run. The Marines were too far away to hear the plunge of the 2,000 lb JDAM. There was no doubt when it impacted, though. A huge gout of smoke reached into the sky, and a few moments later, the sound wave reached across the valley.

"Warheads on their foreheads is right. Well, do we ask for another strike? This is your ball game, not mine," Manny asked.

Without eyes on target, there was no way to know if the varg pack had been hit, or hit hard enough to stop their planned assault.

"Yeah," Aiden said with sudden conviction.

As Manny had said, "in for a penny."

"Another strike, a little farther west."

"Away from Charlie One, sure. A grunt corporal overturning an Army commander. What could be more normal?" Manny asked, but he sent in the nine-line.

It took awhile for the big B-1 up there somewhere to turn around for another bomb run. But it dropped two bombs this time, and it seemed as if half of the high ground over there simply disintegrated.

Whatever had sent his nerves twisting and turning before disintegrated as well. Just as assuredly has he had known that it was a varg pack going to wipe out the village, he now knew the threat was gone. As tough as a varg is, it just can't stand up to the best the US Air Force could throw at it.

Aiden felt at peace. Personally, he could be in deep kimchi, even facing brig time. He had just essentially commandeered two aircraft for something other than a Coalition mission. But he was OK with that. He'd scramble to explain himself to the major and hope the senior officer could cover him, but if not, so be it.

Given the same situation, he wouldn't have changed a thing.

Chapter 21

Nikolai Borisov was livid, and it took all of the self-control he developed in his 72 years of life to keep from shifting and running berserk among those unlucky enough to be near him. It was bad enough that he'd lost so many of his fighters, but the entire Council would soon know, and that could ruin him. This would cost him prestige, but it could also cost him his life. And if no one on the Council challenged him, then one of the young cubs in his own tribe might feel confident enough to challenge him for his position as the Alpha.

Not that he thought anyone in his tribe could take him. He'd been careful to arrange for "accidents" or other means to remove those he thought could pose a threat later as they gained in maturity. The danger in that was that he was now surrounded by incompetents, the very ones he deemed incapable of ever posing a threat.

He simmered with suppressed fury as he waited for his lieutenant, for Rustam, that incompetent worm, to make his way to him. How that piece of slime managed to survive the debacle was something Nikolai dearly wanted to find out.

Finally, the ancient cedar doors swung open and Rustam, along with two others, made their way down the long empty room to where Nikolai sat on his chair like some ancient king. He even had the requisite attendants on either side of him.

Nikolai wrinkled his nose as the smell of fear hit him. Even in human form, the worm reeked of it. Nikolai was amazed that Rustam could even stay on his feet, the panic was so evident.

This is one of my trusted lieutenants? he wondered. Maybe I'm paying the price for getting rid of all my good ones.

"So tell me," he began without bothering with any niceties, "how did you manage to lose 80 vargs and human fighters to a pack of mongrel ferals?"

"But I told you, Nikolai, it wasn't the tribe. We were attacked from the skies. It rained fire on us. Only ten of us made it out alive, and two of them were humans."

Nikolai didn't have to ask what happened to the two humans.

"And somehow, you managed to be one of the survivors?"

"I was in the front, Nikolai, and the planes hit us from behind. All of us who survived were leading the pack," he protested, barely getting it out.

Nikolai let that go, instead switching to, "A plane attacked you. Why, and how was a plane so effective against you?"

"I don't know. The first time, it was gunfire. Some of us fell, but not all. We thought it was over, and we started to continue, but then the whole world exploded. I was thrown into the air and suffered broken bones. Almost all of us who survived were hurt, and the rest, those in back of us, some we couldn't find anything left of them," Rustam said, stammering through most of it.

"You had ten left, and you didn't press on?" Nikolai asked, disdain dripping from his words.

He wouldn't have expected the small force to continue with the attack, but he needed to cement his expectations to the rest of his tribe. He would accept nothing less than total success.

"No, Nikolai, we were hurt and needed to heal. And we didn't know if the enemy would return. We . . . I . . . we needed to let you know what happened," he said hurriedly.

"How considerate. Letting me know. I think when all of you disappeared, I would have known you had failed and lost your worthless lives.

"So, *Rustam*," he started, almost making the name sound like an insult, "why were you hit by airplanes? How did you screw up, and whose airplanes were they?"

"Nikolai, I kept us a long ways from the Americans. It had to be them. They have a small base farther down the valley, and we could sense a small team in the area, but far away from us. We were careful, I swear it!"

"Not careful enough, evidently. You had a simple mission, one even a half-grown cub could accomplish. You failed in it. You cost me 50 fighting vargs and more humans. More than that, you cost me my honor. That is unforgivable."

Nikolai stood up and shifted, letting his *ishton* fall to the ground. As he took his form, he felt his rage build up.

Rustam squeaked like a mouse and immediately shifted as well, only his clothing, while loose enough to accommodate the shift, hung up on him, almost as if binding him to await Nikolai's displeasure.

Nikolai bounded forward at his hapless lieutenant. Rustam's fear pervaded the room, and that excited Nikolai. Rustam immediately fell on the floor, back down, and tilted his head and exposing his throat, the posture of total submission, of total surrender.

Nikolai felt the ingrained hesitation as some of his rage faded. His kind were hard-wired to accept this surrender, accept their dominance over the other. It was simple species survival. If every disagreement ended in death for one, the Tribe would have disappeared long ago. With his total surrender, Rustam was saving his worthless life by acknowledging Nikolai's complete and utter, well, almost *ownership* over him.

Nikolai looked down at the exposed throat, and for a moment, he wavered. But he hadn't gotten to the top by being weak. Almost every other alpha would have accepted such a submission, keeping his or her pack stronger by not diminishing it by a member. Nikolai was not every other alpha, however. He could override his genetic instincts.

With an almost orgasmic thrill, he sank his teeth into Rustam's exposed throat, tearing most of it out with one massive bite. Rustam's blood filled his senses as it flowed down his throat. He felt invigorated, as if he was absorbing Rustam's very essence.

Rustam was dead—he just didn't know it yet. His body jerked as his brain kept sending urgent messages to breathe, not realizing that most of his trachea no longer existed. What was left at the base of the throat was blocked with torn tissue and blood.

There was still the spark of cognizance in Rustam's eyes as he looked up at Nikolai. Even then, knowing his life was ebbing away, there was no anger, no fight in him. When he had surrendered, it had been total. Nikolai sneered at his soon-to-be-former lieutenant. That was the difference between an alpha and the rest. He would never have surrendered. Sometime in the future—the far future, he hoped—when some young varg challenged him, and they fought lycan to lycan, he would lose his life, but it would not be an easy victory for the new alpha. Nikolai would go fighting until the last, never giving up.

Nikolai licked his fangs, tasting the blood. Almost casually, he reached out and put his hand on Rustam's muzzle. Rustam stared at him through Nikolai's splayed claws, surrender still in his eyes. Nikolai shifted his grip, putting his hand inside Rustam's mouth. With a dying bite, Rustam could take off Nikolai's hand, yet he didn't. Somewhere deep inside of him, he wished Rustam could dredge up the gumption to bite, to prove to Nikolai that choosing him for one of his lieutenants had not been a mistake. But it was not the closing to Rustam's jaw that he felt—it was Rustam's tongue, softly licking his hand like some sort of dog.

That rekindled the fire burning within him. With his knee on Rustam's chest, anchoring him, Nikolai grabbed Rustam's jaw and snapped it off. He flung the mandible to the side, then with both hands, took Rustam by the sides of his head and jerked the head off the flopping body. More blood arched in the air as he threw the head across the room.

It was done. He slowly stood up, leaving Rustam's quivering body where it lay. He looked to the others in the room. Not one of them caught his eye.

Cowards!

He'd made his point, though, and the knowledge that even total surrender would not save one of them from his wrath would spread through the remaining tribe.

"Doniyor, you will now take over for Rustam. Do not fail me. Your first task will be to extract revenge for this. We let the Coalition and the Taliban play their games as long as they left us alone. Now, if they want to get into our business, that is their mistake. Find out if it was the Americans, and if it was, then hit them. Make them pay."

The stink of fear that had been radiating from Doniyor faded as he realized that he was not going to die, at least not just yet. He had to attack human soldiers, but that was a far better fate than facing Nikolai's wrath.

Nikolai watched Doniyor as he hurried from the room. On the floor, Rustam's body had stopped quivering. Nikolai looked at it dispassionately for a moment before signaling to one of the others to clear it away. He could have let Rustam live, he knew, but part of being an alpha, particularly a long-living alpha, was to instill fear in his tribe. Killing Rustam helped buttress that fear among the tribe. Now, he had to instill that same kind of fear in the Americans. They would learn to leave him and his alone.

Chapter 22

SFC Jeff Douglas watched as his target stepped out and into the latrine, a roll of toilet paper in hand. This was going to be easier than he thought.

Jeff was not the name he'd been born with, nor was he a sergeant first class in the Army, but he'd had so many different identities in the past that it was like changing clothes, nothing more. It would do. The name and rank had gotten him on the resupply bird, where he'd delivered some real, if superfluous, papers to the FOB commander, and now he was free to perform his real mission.

He waited a few moments, scanning the area. It was clear, so without hesitation, he walked up and slipped into the room. His target's body armor was there on its tree, easily accessible. Jeff pulled it off and laid it on the floor, opening it to expose the inside. With an economy of motion, he slit the bottom of the fabric along the seam with his X-ACTO knife and then slid in what looked to be a thick piece of duct tape. It sealed easily to the back of the Kevlar panel. Using a small tube of a powerful adhesive, he closed back up the seam where he'd opened it. It wasn't a perfect closure, but he doubted anyone would notice it.

All of this took less than a minute, Jeff noted with satisfaction. His practice back in Kabul had paid off. He put the gear back on the tree and with confidence, stepped out of the room. It was better to move boldly than to open the door a crack and peek out. No one was in sight, so he turned to go to the tent where he'd been temporarily assigned. Half of his mission was over, and he had time to kill, so he might as well catch some shut-eye.

He didn't wonder about his target or what he'd done to have Jeff assigned to him. He tried never to think of them—any of his targets—as people. Usually, in this latest persona, he'd targeted Afghans and the occasional Pakistani or Uzbek, but as had been throughout his career, his targets had occasionally been Americans. Whether they deserved his attention or not was something he didn't consider. He received his orders and acted on them. He wasn't particularly pleased when his target was US military—long ago, he'd served a tour with the Army, first as a grunt and then with the Special Forces. But he'd had so many personas since then that it was hard to remember just who he really was at times. Whatever this guy had done was between him and Jeff's handlers.

It was mid-morning, and the transient tent was empty. Jeff pulled up his pack to use as a pillow and laid down. Within a minute, he was asleep.

Chapter 23

"What the hell?" Cree asked, pointing up to the ledge some 200 feet above them and 150 feet back as they marched down the trail. "That's freakin' amazing!"

Aiden had felt their presence for some time now, so he wasn't surprised. He wasn't worried, either. This time, the lycan spoor posed no threat, of that he was positive. Looking up to where Cree was pointing, he saw the three of them. He recognized Zakia immediately, and a thrill swept through him. He had to resist the urge to grovel like a pup happy to see its master come home. He didn't recognize the two who stood behind and to each side of her, but they had to be from the village.

"Holy shit!" Mike said as he looked up. "Look at the size of them. I thought the wolves here in these mountains were little things, no bigger than coyotes. Those look like timber wolves."

"There ain't no timber wolves here," Cree said. "There's some big ones up in Russia, but that's a long way away."

"Russia or not, those are some big mother fuckers," Mike said. "It's creepy the way they're looking at us, though, like we are lunch on the hoof."

The team continued to walk on the trail below the lycans as the three of them silently watched the Marines. All of the Marines kept looking up, amazed at the brazen nature of the "wolves."

As Aiden came abreast of the lycans, the two behind Zakia stepped back out of sight while Zakia pushed her forepaws out and lowered her muzzle to the ground.

"Did you see that? It's like it's bowing to us!" Cree exclaimed, louder than he should be while still out in Indian Country.

"No shit, even the wildlife knows we're the kings of this fucking jungle," Rob said from behind Aiden. "I hope Brett gets that on his camera. I want to Facebook that."

Brett doubled as the team's combat photographer. He was farther back in the column, but if he could see the lycans, he almost assuredly would be taking photos.

Aiden wheeled around to look for Brett. He didn't think having a photo of a lycan online, where some expert could see it and recognize something was wrong, was a good idea.

Zakia had closed her eyes as she showed deference, but with her muzzle still down, she opened them and stared at Aiden as he looked back up at her. Despite the distance between them, he knew she was thanking him.

How the hell she knew he had interceded for her tribe, Aiden didn't know. There was still too much about his new life that he didn't understand, so he wasn't particularly surprised. He hadn't planned on announcing what he'd done for them, but deep in his heart, he was glad they knew. He really, *really* wanted Zakia's approval.

As soon as their eyes met, Zakia pushed back up, spun around, and disappeared out of sight.

"That was like on Discovery Channel!" Cree said, still looking up the cliff face. "Cool as shit!"

It *was* pretty cool, Aiden thought, although none of his team would believe the truth of what had just happened in a million years.

Chapter 24

The team had been back for a day, and Aiden had delayed meeting with the major. He wasn't quite sure how much he'd tell him. He'd never told anyone yet, not even his mother. Now, he owed MAJ Ward something. The question was how much he should reveal.

He didn't even think he could approach Hozan on it. Hozan was his friend, his confidant. Aiden had told Hozan about Zakia giving him deference, and while Hozan knew that Aiden had instigated the air strike, to him it was no big deal. As bright as Hozan was, as much as he acted as a mentor to Aiden, he didn't have a clue as to the inner workings of the military and thought nothing of a grunt corporal calling in two Air Force birds, especially after the mission had initially been disapproved.

Aiden had been on tenterhooks from the moment he got back, expecting to answer for what he'd done, but no one had said a word after the debrief. Evidently, the major had already blocked any inquiry into that. That still left the Army officer, though, waiting for Aiden's explanation.

He desperately wanted to know just how much the major, or the mysterious higher-ups, knew about him. He wanted to hold as much back as possible, but unless he knew what they knew, he had the potential to mess up pretty badly.

Aiden squared his shoulders and pushed open the door to the major's small office. Both the major and the specialist looked up as he came in, but after the major nodded at him, the specialist, whose name Aiden couldn't get straight, got up and left the office. Aiden moved over and took his seat. He sat there a moment, trying to gather his thoughts.

Finally, he just said, "I have to thank you, sir, for getting that air strike. You saved a lot of people with that."

Well, werewolves, he thought.

"I put my ass on the line for that," MAJ Ward said. "I trust it was worth it?"

"Yes, sir!" he answered hurriedly. "It was a righteous mission, one that was needed."

It might have been his unrehearsed earnestness in his reply that the major saw, because he waited a moment, then nodded, seemingly accepting his statement at face value—for now, at least.

"So . . ." the major said to a pregnant pause.

"Um, sir, I know I told you I had something to say. It's hard to explain it though, and even harder to believe. There's this program, sir, an experiment, some sort of super soldier thing. I don't think I'm supposed to tell anyone about it, only that I get tested and stuff. I don't even know who else is in the program. All I know is that sometimes, I feel like Superman. I'm stronger and faster than I was before, so I think this experiment is working. I think the best thing to do would be to show you sometime, so you can see. But I've got to ask you, sir, to keep this quiet. They told me this was Top Secret."

Fuck, that sounded like bullshit, Aiden acknowledged to himself as he looked intently into the major's eyes to see if he'd bought it.

MAJ Ward was emotionless as he stared back at Aiden. "And when did this experiment take place?"

"After I got wounded, sir. I wasn't too gung ho, then, sir, and not that great of a Marine, to be honest. I think they wanted to take me because anything would be an improvement."

Aiden was glad he'd rehearsed that answer. He thought by criticizing his former self, it might sound more real. Not many Marines went around talking themselves down to others.

"So you can't talk about it, but you can show me?" the major asked.

"Well, sir, no one never said nohow I couldn't show anyone, just not talk about it. So, maybe I can do it first, then ask permission later."

Aiden waited anxiously to hear the major's response. Would he buy it? Did he know more, and was about to call Aiden out on his fantasy story?

"OK, there corporal, you're on. You set the time, and we'll see what you can do."

Chapter 25

Private First Class Jordan Lestair kept watch, scanning the approaches to the little Godforsaken collection of huts that served as a village in the Hindu Kush. He was a trunk monkey[40] for the mission, manning the Humvee's .50 cal Ma Deuce. With Corporal Chris Lin, they comprised the security element responsible to the east of the village. Larry and Ponce were in another Humvee on the road leading to the northwest out of the village.

There was an ANA platoon also providing security, but Jordan not only didn't give them much credence, he also actively did not trust them. There had been too many green-on-blue attacks in the country, and Jordan spent most of his time surveilling them as well as the small ANP guard shack with its three ANPs. The Taliban were more obvious targets. They came at you, and you shot them. The ANA and ANP would turn on a soldier in a second, switching from so-called friend to enemy.

Behind him, the rest of the platoon was in position to secure the small hut where the captain, the lieutenant, and some other O[41] from battalion were conferring with the village elders. They were probably sipping tea and acting like the hajji's best friends, even though everyone knew they were all Taliban. Second platoon had taken fire from around here only two weeks ago, and now, everyone was acting like best buds.

Jordan shook his head. He was infantry. He hoped to become a Ranger. His job was to kill the enemy, not play footsie with them. He was glad that was left to the Os.

"How much longer are they gonna be?" he asked Lin.

Lin was somewhat of an asshole, but he was a proficient asshole, and for Jordan, that made him a good partner when out beyond the wire. He could count on Lin.

---

[40] Trunk Monkey: slang for the turret gunner on a vehicle.
[41] O: slang for officer.

"Fuck if I know," Lin said from below him from the Humvee's driver's seat.

This was supposed to be a two-hour powwow, but it had already stretched out to four, and dusk was closing in. There was a good chance that the captain would have them bivvy back down the jumbled dirt road they'd come up for the night rather than try and make the two hours back to the FOB in the darkness. The road was barely more than a trail, and in some places, going off it meant a long fall down the mountainside.

"Everything OK?" Staff Sergeant Galloway asked from behind the Humvee.

Galloway was Jordan's squad leader. Most of the squad was situated around and on the roof of one of the huts, but with Jordan and Lin out front, he checked on them every 30 minutes or so.

"Nothing much happening," Lin said, a second too soon.

While Jordan was watching, a dark shape bolted into the ANP guardshack. Before whatever it was could register with him, shouts and an unearthly growling erupted from inside the flimsy wooden structure. The shouts turned into terror-filled screaming before being cut off.

"What the fuck?" Jordan asked as he swung his Ma Deuce to cover the shack.

Something big and round flew out of the opening in the guard shack that served as a window. It hit the ground and rolled as Jordan instinctively covered it. As it came to a rest, the flat, unseeing eyes stared out from the decapitated head that had been attached to the rest of the ANP's body only moments before.

The hajji soldiers in the ANA squad who were just back from the guardshack jumped up and stared dumbly at the head. One or two started edging back towards the center of the village when a soul-shattering howl filled the night, quickly joined by another.

The ANA hajjis broke and ran, dropping their weapons in their panic to get away. Two were not quick enough. Dark shapes burst out of the shack and tackled two of the slower Afghan soldiers. Jordan brought his Ma Deuce on one of them, but the *thing* had stood up with the hapless soldier in its grasp, the soldier between Jordan and whatever was attacking him.

"Lin, where's Jacobs?" he asked, referring to the squad's advanced marksman. "I don't have a shot!"

Jordan didn't like any Afghans, and he didn't trust the ANA, but he was not about to blow one of them apart.

It didn't make any difference. The creature bit around the hajji's neck, and the head came off. Jordan leveled a burst of fire. The Ma Deuce's big 655-grain rounds could bring down an elephant, and Jordan instinctively knew, just as Homo erectus knew when the saber tooths were roaming outside the cave, that he had to fight or die.

But with an unbelievable quickness, the thing was gone, and Jordan's rounds punched out into the trees. Every hair on Jordan's body stood on end as he searched for targets.

Not every ANA was running away. Unbelievably, one of them was running forward, passing Jordan's Humvee as he ran to meet the nightmares. It was the ANA lieutenant, a grizzled veteran of the war with the Soviets. He had out a shining foot-and-a-half knife, the one Jordan had seen in a sheath strapped to his thigh.

Beneath him, both Lin and SSGT Galloway were firing their M16s. They were impacting on a shape in the fading light, and while Jordan couldn't make out its features well, it looked like some big fucking dog, but one standing on its hind legs. It rose from a dead ANA, and Jordan swore he could see red eyes glaring at the three Americans. It burst into a charge as Jordan swung his Ma Deuce around.

It was quick, fucking quick, and it was two steps away from the Humvee when Jordan pulled the trigger. Within seconds, 15 rounds blasted the thing apart, showering the three with blood and gore.

"Fire, fire!" the heavily accented ANA lieutenant was shouting back.

As Jordan swung around to acquire the target, he was stunned to see the lieutenant standing up to another monster, jabbing at it with his silvery knife. Jordan expected the thing to destroy the foolhardy lieutenant, but it actually seemed wary as it feinted several times at the Afghan.

"Fire!" the lieutenant screamed again.

Whatever it was, it was taller than the lieutenant—taller, but not by much, and Jordan knew he could easily hit him if he fired.

It's your funeral, he thought as he pulled the trigger.

The Ma Deuce reached out, almost taking the top of the lieutenant's head off as Jordan nailed his attacker right in the forehead. The top half of the thing's head disappeared in an explosion of red.

Jordan felt a jolt of pride. That was a difficult shot with a Ma Deuce, but he smoked the thing while a friendly was right in front of it. To his surprise, the lieutenant wasn't done but fell on the twitching body. With several hacks at the neck, he cut off what remained of the head.

Talk about crazy fucks! he thought.

"Jordan, at your eleven!" Galloway shouted.

Jordan tore his eyes away from the lieutenant as he brandished his bloody trophy. In the trees on the other side of the road, about 40 meters away, several sets of red eyes stared out of the deepening darkness. ROE be fucked—Jordan didn't hesitate. He opened up, sending round after round into the trees. When he stopped, his barrel smoking hot, the eyes were gone.

"Holy shit," Lin said from the side of the Humvee, where he had his M16 out. "What the fuck was all of this?"

They ignored the radio asking for an update as they stared blankly at the scene before them. Jordan silently watched the ANA lieutenant as he went to the second body and hacked the head off the mangled torso.

"A little overkill?" Lin asked from beneath him.

By that time, the rest of the squad had arrived. SSGT Galloway ordered Brent Miller, Sergeant Brent Miller, the first team leader, to check the bodies of the two dead, well, attackers.

The three soldiers waited as the team went forward to where the ANA lieutenant was standing by the first body. The lieutenant stepped aside as Miller came up.

"He's fucking smoked, in pieces. You shot his clothes right off!" Miller shouted back.

He? No clothes? Jordan had expected an "it" at the least. Whatever that was, it was not human, that was for sure.

"It's human?" Galloway shouted out, obviously of the same mind as Jordan.

"Not anymore," Miller shouted back.

"This one's naked, too!" Bunky shouted out from where he stood over Jordan's head shot. "His head's gone, but the rest of him is fine, just stark naked."

"What the fuck?" SSGT Galloway said, confused. "Lestair, what did you see?"

Jordan knew what he saw. Evidently, his squad leader saw the same thing. But Miller and Bunky, they were seeing dead, if naked, hajjis, nothing more. Was this one of those mass hallucination things? Was he going crazy?

He chose to be noncommittal. "Uh, I don't know, Staff. I just fired. I couldn't see anything clearly."

"You didn't see those things?" Lin asked accusingly.

"Sorry, I just fired."

"Hey, Cubbie!" Galloway shouted out for their terp.

Jordan never remembered Cubbie's real name. He was "Cubbie" to everyone due to his love of the Chicago Cubs, despite never having seen them play, even on television.

"Ask that lieutenant what the fuck just happened," Galloway told their interpreter.

Cubbie went forward to where the lieutenant was checking on his dead soldiers. Jordan could see five of them littering the ground like broken dolls. There had been four ANP in the guardshack, and while Jordan could only see one of their heads from where it had been thrown, he was pretty sure all of them had been killed. That was nine dead on their side, two, maybe more among the attackers. "Attackers" seemed too generic, but deep inside, Jordan knew they weren't mujahideen.

Jordan watched as Cubbie approached the lieutenant. ANA or not, that was one hard-ass motherfucker. Jordan had been about shitting in his trou, and he was in back of a Ma Deuce. He knew he'd been only seconds from joining the dead ANA soldiers before he was able to blow that fucking thing away. Yet that lieutenant had run into the battle armed with a friggin' knife, for Pete's sake. A knife!

111

Cubbie talked to the lieutenant for a few moments, then came back to Galloway. "Lieutenant Wafa Khan thanks you for your help. Now he must take care of his dead," he told them.

"But who the fuck were they?" Galloway insisted.

"He says that is not for us to worry about. He will take care of it."

"Cubbie! I want some answers!" Galloway insisted.

"I am sorry, Staff Sergeant. But the lieutenant, he is, what you might call, a 'hunter.' Most of us here in the mountains, we don't believe in the old tales. But we still don't question those who call themselves that."

"What the hell is a hunter?" Lin asked.

"I . . . I have said too much. Please, forget it. It is an old tradition, like you say, an old wives tale. I am a modern man, so forgive me if I fell back into superstition," he said before hurrying off before he could be questioned further.

Somewhere in their DNA was the gene that feared the darkness, that knew there were monsters beyond the reach of the light of the campfire. That gene reared its ugly head as Jordan listened. The three soldiers watched as the remains of what looked to be normal men were carried past them before they agreed to say nothing about their mutual hallucination. But Jordan knew that was a lie, and when the squad reported that there was blood just inside the treeline, but no body, Jordan shuddered. Nothing stood up to a .50 cal and ran off.

Whatever had attacked them, Jordan really didn't want to know. He'd let that crazy "hunter" deal with it and hope the attackers would stay out of his dreams at night.

Chapter 26

Lomri Baridman Gorbat Wafa Khan, who the Americans referred to as "Lieutenant Wafa Khan," oversaw the loading of his men's bodies onto the beat-up truck that would take them down the mountain.

He cared for his men, and he mourned their passing, yet he was filled with exultation. He was not just an Army officer. He came from a long line of *shkaarzan*, of hunters. Some knew them as *lewan-shkaarzan*, but it wasn't the animal *lewan*—wolves—they hunted, but darker creatures. As his people were dragged into the 21st Century, many of the old traditions died as the young wanted cell phones and televisions. But here in the mountains, far from the cities, some still held to the old ways. Some believed in the *Shaytan* spawn that tried to destroy men and hasten the end of days.

Gorbat's father had been a *shkaarzan*, and his father before him, and yet his father before him, and so on reaching far back into their past. Gorbat had clung to his training, his beliefs, despite never encountering a *ghuul*, as the creatures were known in the old Arabic texts, or *wargalewa* in his own native Pashto. He knew they were out there, biding their time to bring about the end of times. He'd served in the Army, first under the warlords fighting the Soviet invaders, now with the new invaders. It didn't really make much difference to him who he fought. He tried to keep his men alive while watching for the *wargalewa*. He was born to protect his people, the Pashtun, and that was what drove him.

Then today, in this small mountain village, the spawn came forth. When they hit the police station, he immediately recognized what they were. He'd never heard one before, never seen one, but that didn't matter. Without hesitation, he charged, his silver *pesh-kabz*[42] drawn and ready for battle. Confronting *Shaytan's* minion filled him with elation. He didn't believe in the promise to martyrs

---

[42] *Pesh-kabz*: a traditional knife developed in Iran and Afghanistan originally designed to penetrate armor.

of 72 virgins in heaven, but he imagined that this was how those men felt as they pulled the pin on their suicide vests. He was filled with a holy presence as he fought for Allah.

The creature was taller than him, and from what he'd witnessed, ungodly strong, but it recognized the presence of a warrior of Allah. It hesitated, wary of his holy *pesh-kabz*. Despite his fervor, though, Gorbat was a practical man, and the Americans had weapons, too. The soldier on the .50 caliber gun had sent one of the minions back to hell already, so in his somewhat broken English, Gorbat ordered him to open fire on the devil facing him. The soldier didn't hesitate, and Gorbat felt the big rounds blast over his head, a shock wave caused by the rounds' passing. One hit the *wargalewa* high on the forehead, taking it off the top of its vile head in an explosion of blood, brains, and bone.

Gorbat knew that the creatures were tough and hard to kill. He wasn't sure if losing half of its head was enough, however. He was taught early on in his training that the only sure way to keep one of them dead was to remove its head completely, so that is what he did. The *pesh-kabz* was not designed for sawing, nor was silver the best metal for a blade, but that is what a *shkaarzan* was required to use.

When the fight was over, at least two of the *wargalewa* were dead. There had been more, waiting out in the trees, but they had been driven off by the American on the Humvee. With his senses attuned, he knew that at least one more had been hit but not killed. The rest got away, and Gorbat's blood pumped hotly as he realized he had a renewed mission. He would not rest until he returned every *meanong*[43] *wargalewa* in these mountains to *Shaytan* in hell.

---

[43] *Meanong*: Pashto for son or daughter of a dog

Chapter 27

Hozan was with Aiden when the Army platoon returned to the FOB. This was nothing of note, but the truck with the dead bodies was an indication that they'd seen action. Hozan had seen many bodies during his years, and he didn't pay these too much attention until a faint whiff tickled his senses.

He held up his hand, silencing whatever Aiden was about to say while he focused on the eight, no, nine bodies being lowered from the vehicle. They had been wrapped in ponchos, but it was obvious that they had suffered severe trauma. That was not what caught Hozan's attention, though. It was the very faint presence of varg that enveloped them. He doubted that too many others could discern the spoor, especially from 70 meters away, but Hozan had always had better senses concerning the Tribe than others.

These men had been killed by vargs, no question about it. This could be bad, very bad, and Hozan wondered if this could be related to the killing of the varg attack force. If so, this could have serious ramifications. He looked at his young friend and hoped that no one from the Tribe knew of his part in the bombing that had saved Zakia's tribe, but killed others of their kind.

One of the ANA officers came back to supervise the unloading of the bodies. Immediately, every hair on Hozan's body rose, and he had to fight back the urge to shift. Without a doubt, this man was the enemy. Aiden's yet poorly developed senses couldn't pick it up, but Hozan knew what this man was.

Over the years, Hozan's kind had had the advantage over the humans. They could kill humans at will without repercussion. However, the pernicious humans would not give up and simply be helpless prey. Certain groups of people banded together to fight off the threat. Different cultures developed these men, these hunters of the Tribe, in different ways. But they evolved in a similar fashion. Some went down dead ends, using superstitious talismans and protections in their fight. They ended up dead. But by trial and error, those that survived taught others what they did to survive, and the body of knowledge grew. Distance kept them from full integration with each other, and some groups were more effective than others, but the survivors, the hunters, could sometimes defeat those of the Tribe.

The same sense that enabled Hozan to detect the slightest sign of a shift or presence of one of the Tribe seemed also to be attuned to hunters. Hozan had never seen one in Iraq or the old Soviet Union, he'd never seen one on his pilgrimage to Germany, but here in the Hindu Kush, one was standing there, not 70 meters away.

As Hozan stared, the man suddenly stopped and turned, as if trying to find something. His gaze did not pause as it swept past the two of them, but Hozan was suddenly sure he knew there were two of the Tribe in the area.

"Come," he said to Aiden, taking his friend by the arm and leading him back between the buildings and out of sight.

This was a new development, one he should report back to Nemir. The hunter could be a threat, to Hozan, certainly, but more to Aiden. As much as his young friend's development as a varg surprised him, he was still a novice with much to learn. A skilled hunter might be more than a match for him.

Chapter 28

Aiden kept scanning the terrain, looking for any sign of danger. He pushed his senses as far as he could, his imagination going rampant. Not only did he have to worry about the Taliban, not only was there a werewolf war going on, but now Hozan told him there was some sort of hunter on the loose, a human whose mission it was to take down werewolves.

Aiden wanted to dismiss the last one, but Hozan had assured him the danger was real. A varg was much more powerful than a human, yet Aiden had used human weapons to take out the attack on the village. He was only now beginning to realize that being a werewolf was not a free pass when it came to a fight. Still, he wasn't sure what a single Afghan could do even against a newbie varg such as himself.

To make matters worse, MAJ Ward was along with the mission, sitting in Aiden's GMV. This was only the team's second mission mounted in the GMVs, and Aiden was the trunk monkey for the middle vehicle. When the orders came down to escort the major on a mission of "observation," Norm had immediately put him with Aiden. It seemed that the major was to be his charge. Major Ward had taken a brief moment when they were almost alone to whisper to Aiden that the mission was from on high, and he was supposed to covertly observe Aiden in action. So Aiden had Taliban, other members of the Tribe, some Afghan werewolf hunter, and now his own country's higher command on his ass.

At least the major had been open about it. Aiden realized that the major could just be playing a game to gain his trust, but Aiden sensed the major was solid. He was on Aiden's side, so to speak.

Aiden was concerned about taking the man out beyond the wire, however. The guy only had one leg, for Pete's sake. Granted, it was barely noticeable, but that was back at the FOB. Out here, in the mountains, was no place for a one-legged man. No matter what high-tech leg the Army had given him, he could not be as able as he should be. Even most whole-bodied Marines couldn't keep up with the team, much less one with a physical disability.

He risked a glance down the gun turret at the major. They were about three hours from the FOB, a bouncing, jarring three-hour ride. But the major had wedged himself into the small seat and was seemingly coping.

The team was heading for a high point where the entire valley could be observed. This mission was bullshit, and everyone knew it. If there really was a reason for the major to get a feel of the valley, a simple helo lift would have sufficed with much less effort. Only Aiden knew the real reason for the mission.

He hadn't yet showed the major his enhanced abilities—as a human. He hadn't the opportunity, to be sure, but he wasn't pushing it, either. And the major seemed OK with that. But matters had been taken out of his hands, if he was telling the truth. No matter, even without the major's warning, what with all the other crazy things happening around him, Aiden was not about to shift anytime soon.

After another 20 minutes, the three vehicles pulled to a stop in the treeline. Off to the left, about 30 meters away, the mountainside opened up, providing the views over the valley.

Norm dismounted and came up to Aiden's GMV. "OK, you and Rob, escort the major to the vantage point while we set up security.

"Major, if you'll follow Corporal Kaas and Sergeant Christianson, they'll take you to where you can do what you have to. If possible, though, I'd like to leave here for the second point within 30 minutes, sir."

"No problem, Lieutenant. This shouldn't take long," MAJ Ward said as he clambered out of the GMV.

He took one odd hop, but other than that, he showed no sign of having a prosthetic. For this vantage point, it would be an easy walk. The next one would be more difficult with a bit of a climb.

The rest of the team moved into position to provide security while the major said, "Lead on, Sergeant."

This was military form. Rob was senior to Aiden, so the major was right to address him. However, everyone was well aware by now that there was some sort of connection between Aiden and the major. They just chose to ignore it. Aiden hadn't sensed any resentment or distrust, but he was afraid of it. A team had to have total trust and confidence in each other if it was to be effective in combat.

Within a minute, the three men stepped up to the flat rock that offered spectacular views over the valley. Despite himself, Aiden had to stop to take it in. The team had had many missions down there, but from here, it looked peaceful and serene. In the far distance the haze smoothed out the mountainsides, but from the point down to the bottom of the valley, the air was crisp and clear. The sharp smell of evergreens flooded Aiden's senses. It was hard to believe at that moment that the area was at war.

Chapter 29

SFC Jeff Douglas watched the three men walk out onto the vantage point. He wasn't surprised. He'd been told where they would be and on what day. It had taken him two days to hike to his present position, a lone American in the mountains of Afghanistan, but he'd never felt threatened. He could have just as easily been hiking the Sierra Nevada Trail.

For the briefest moment, he wondered why his target was chosen. What had the man done? He quickly pushed that aside, though. He had done a lot of shit in his life, and he had quickly discovered that it didn't pay to humanize his targets. Sure, this one was American, but a man was a man, his blood red like everyone else's. He didn't make any life-or-death decisions. He was merely a tool, and instrument to implement those decisions.

His hide was almost 250 meters away, well within range. Without hesitation, he pulled the transmitter out of its carrying case, armed it, and pressed the trigger.

Chapter 30

Aiden was still transfixed by the view when a muffled *whump* sounded beside him. He turned to look to see Major Ward fall to the ground.

Shit! I knew he'd be a liability!

He started to bend to help him up when the smell hit him—the smell of blood and feces. At the same time, he realized that the major's leg hadn't failed him. The man was down hard, curling into the fetal position. Aiden hadn't heard a sniper's shot, but something had hit the man.

Rob was already on the radio calling to Doc as Aiden reached for the major, turning him on his back. The major's flak jacket seemed whole, but blood was beginning to flow from beneath it.

From beneath it?

Aiden started to undo the Velcro fastening on the front of the flak jacket, but as he caught sight of the twisted mess *inside* the body armor, he quickly fastened it back up. It was the only thing holding the major together.

"Major, are you with me?" he shouted, taking his hand and squeezing it. "Hold on, sir!"

MAJ Ward was gasping for breath, his eyes rolled up in his head, his skin already turning the sickly gray cast of rotten liver. This was serious.

"Doc's coming," Rob said, looking over Aiden's shoulder. "How the fuck did he get hit inside his flak jacket?" he asked. "No booby trap does that!"

Aiden didn't know what to say. Still holding the major's hand, he looked up, willing Doc to get there quicker. The major was about gone, but maybe Doc could stabilize him somehow until he could get into surgery.

The major gurgled horribly as his blood worked its way up his throat.

Aiden stared at the man in horror. He was going to die, right here on the mountainside.

"Let me see," Doc said as he rushed up, pushing Aiden aside.

"What happened?" Norm asked right behind him.

"We don't know. We were just standing here when there was a kind of sound, like a fart, and then the major was down. But he was hit inside his flak jacket, not outside," Rob told him, his words coming out in a rush.

"That's impossible. Something penetrated the jacket, then expanded," Norm said.

"No, sir," Rob said, reverting to sergeant and lieutenant. "Check it out. Front and back, no penetration."

"Bullshit, you must have missed it. We'll check it after he's stabilized."

He turned away and called on his radio, "Manny, we need an immediate CASEVAC. Get your ass up here."

"Shit, shit, shit," Doc was saying as he examined the now quiet major.

For a moment, Aiden thought the major had died, but his chest still moved with his struggles to breathe.

"Norm, there's no way," Doc said, looking up at the team leader.

"Until it's over, there's always a way. Stabilize him, then I want the aid station ready for him. If he can last long enough, the surgeons can work miracles."

Doc seemed to consider what to do for a moment before pushing the edges of the major's flak jacket closed.

"Aiden, I want you to put pressure on him, but not too hard. I'm going to see what I can do to keep him alive."

Aiden knew he had a dead man under his hands. Major Ward was already gone—his body just didn't know it yet. Its will to live was strong.

That sickened him. The major had been good to him. He'd told Aiden about the interest in him. He'd put his own career on the line by doing that. Most of all, he'd taken Aiden's word and gone over some heads to get that air strike. If it weren't for the major, Zakia and her tribe would all be dead.

Something told him that whatever had happened to the major, it was because of him. He was the reason. Maybe they'd found out that the major had broken secrecy, and that was his death warrant. The more Aiden thought about it, the more he was positive that this was all related. It was Aiden's fault the major would die.

Fuck that!

Aiden knew that as a kreuzung, he couldn't turn a human. Hozan had been pretty adamant about that. But if Aiden could survive some very serious injuries because of what was coursing through his veins, couldn't that help the major? He wouldn't become a werewolf, but could he borrow Aiden's healing abilities long enough to survive to the field hospital?

He glanced up. Doc was pulling through his medical kit. Norm was on the radio. Rob was looking back, probably watching for Manny.

Aiden bit his tongue as hard as he could. He quickly pulled open the major's flak jacket and spit out the blood that had filled his mouth directly into the mangled mess of what had been the major's gut. He pulled the body armor closed again just as Doc turned back to administer to his patient.

Aiden didn't know what to expect. He wanted Major Ward to open his eyes, to regain consciousness. Neither of those two things happened. He didn't die, either, however. He didn't die when Manny told Norm that somehow, through God knows what kind of foul-up, there were no helos anywhere in theater that could CASEVAC the major. He didn't die as they loaded him in one of the GMVs. He didn't die as they took the long, bouncing drive back to the FOB. He didn't die as they finally got him on a bird to the brigade aid station and onto the operating table.

The word they received some hours later was that the major was going to make it. His injuries were not as bad as they had initially seemed, which got Doc to swearing that was bullshit.

Aiden didn't know one way or the other. The injuries had sure seemed bad at the time. Had he panicked and stupidly spit his blood into a wounded man, or had that blood somehow saved him?

Chapter 31

He's still alive! Interesting, COL Jack Tarniton thought as he read the latest update. *Maybe there's something to this after all.*

That something was not just that Aiden Kaas was a werewolf. The colonel was pretty sure about that. What this might have proved was his personal theory that the same abnormalities that showed up in a werewolf's blood, the abnormalities present in Kaas' blood, were the reason werewolves could heal so readily. And given the varied mythologies surrounding werewolves, it seemed that the blood could instigate a change in humans, to make *them* werewolves.

SFC Douglas, or whatever his real name was, had reported the fatal injury suffered by Ward. The colonel had no reason to doubt that. The operative had come highly recommended and had come up with the method needed to give Ward a fatal injury, but one that kept him alive long enough for Kaas to have the opportunity to save him. That had been the reason he had ordered Ward to become Kaas' friend. Kaas had to care enough about him to do whatever his kind did to humans.

He had only briefly hesitated before taking this path. Ward had been a disappointment as he pushed back against his orders. He should have been grateful for the opportunity. Not many cripples were still on active duty. No one wanted a one-legged infantry officer. The colonel had made a mistake in choosing him, but the past was the past. Ward served his purpose. His injury has flushed out Kaas. The colonel was working for the greater good of the country, and if this was how Ward could serve, then so be it.

Besides, he was going to make it through this alive. And if the colonel was right, he might even become a werewolf himself. The colonel would then have two of them, maybe the first two of many. Imagine what the Army could do with, say, a platoon of warrior werewolves dedicated to the cause?

He wasn't quite ready yet to listen to the siren's call that kept singing in the back of his mind, however. What could he himself do, how far could he go as a werewolf? It was too alluring, so he pushed that back until he could be more sure of the consequences of such a move.

He still had work to do before that possibility could even be considered. He sat down to issue some orders. MAJ Ward was healing surprisingly fast and was about to be CASEVAC'd to Landstuhl.[44] If he was getting better so fast, the colonel wanted him back at FOB Ballenstein with Kaas. Not before a blood sample was taken and sent back to him, of course. He had to see if the good major's blood had been "lycanized," a phrase he'd recently come up with—a damn clever term, if he did say so himself.

Yes, things were going very, very well with him, he noted with satisfaction.

---

[44] Landstuhl: the US Army medical facility in Landstuhl, Germany.

Chapter 32

Hozan was livid. Of all the stupid things Aiden could have done, this was right up there. He loved the young man like a son, but he was about ready to shift and take out the cub's throat himself without waiting for the Council's orders.

"You just killed him," he said to Aiden as his friend stood before him, wringing his hands. "It would have been kinder just to end his suffering."

"He was going to die. His gut was destroyed, and Doc gave him no chance," Aiden protested.

"But he didn't die, did he?"

"Maybe my blood did that? Gave him the strength?"

"I told you about that at Fallujah. You gave me the English term: 'The Xerox Effect.' Remember? You're a kreuzung, not a blood. You cannot change a human. You cannot be a patron. The seed that initiates the change gets attenuated, that is the English word, and will no longer work right."

"I know that, but I hoped that it could give him enough strength to make it to the aid station."

"Your blood did nothing to help him. Not even mine would work that quickly. What it did do is start your major on a long and painful path to death. Your seed does not know it's corrupted, so it will try and force the change. The human's body will fight it. If the human's defenses win, which is what usually happens, the seed self-destructs, poisoning the body and damaging it, and he will die. If your seed somehow is strong enough to win, it cannot initiate the change, and the body destroys itself. This is what you did to him. You have killed him."

"But he's getting better! I've heard the reports! He's even coming back here to the FOB!"

"Humans heal, too. And it takes time for the seed to manifest itself. In two or three weeks, your major will fall ill again as the seed and his body war against each other," Hozan said, watching the pain spread over Aiden's face as he realized what would happen.

Hozan's anger fled. Aiden was a good man, a caring man. He'd come a long way from the self-centered coward he'd been when he'd been bit. Hozan knew that Aiden's patron, Omar Muhmood, almost assuredly had meant to kill Aiden but had been killed himself before he could finish the task. That was a lucky occurrence. Aiden was maturing well, and if the Council let him live, he would be an asset to the Tribe.

"Is there anything we can do?" Aiden asked hopefully.

"We can try to make him comfortable is all. You Americans have many drugs that can ease the pain, and we have opium. We can help ease his passing."

Aiden gave a wordless cry of grief and spun about, rushing to leave the pot shed where they'd been talking. Hozan didn't follow. The world was not a fair place, and despite Aiden's best intentions, he'd sentenced his friend to death. It was a cruel lesson, and one that Hozan hoped would not crush Aiden's spirit.

Chapter 33

To everyone's surprise, Major Ward returned to the FOB a week-and-a-half later. No one had expected to ever see him again. But then he showed up at the FOB LZ, stepping out of the Chinook, albeit a little gingerly.

His battle rattle had been examined, and it was obvious that his flak jacket had been booby-trapped, which led to more suspicions as to the local ANA soldiers. This had the earmarks of a green-on-blue attack. The fact that the major had been singled out actually elevated him in the eyes of the soldiers and Marines on the FOB. No one knew what his and his assistant's mission really was, but if he was targeted like that, it must be pretty important. And for him to come back to the FOB when he'd had his golden ticket back home, well, that was righteous.

Aiden was in turmoil. He had killed the man, he knew. The major had been fucked up, to be sure, but he might have been able to pull through it. Now, he was a dead man walking. He went back and forth in his mind, wanting to take the easy way out and not say anything. When the major got sick as his seed warred with the major's T cells, he could just stay quiet. There were enough exotic diseases in the 'Stan, any one of which could kill a man.

An earlier version of Aiden would have done just that. But since he'd been bit himself, he had gone through a pretty significant transformation. As much as he wanted to stay quiet, he knew he had to inform the major, to tell him what was going to happen.

He waited until the second evening after the major's return. He and Spec Sutikal were in the DFAC when Aiden came in. With his food in hand, he stopped by the major, telling him he wanted to talk, before making his way to where his team was sitting.

An hour later, he went to the major's office. Sutikal was not there, to Aiden's relief.

"Uh, how do you feel?" Aiden asked, feeling stupid and clumsy.

"Surprisingly well, thank you. The docs told me my recovery, my ongoing recovery, is something of a miracle."

"Is there any word on who did this? I mean who wanted to, well . . ."

"Kill me?"

"Uh, yes, sir, I guess so."

"No, not yet. DIA has my gear, and they are going all CIS on it. I'm in the dark about this. I may be the senior soldier in the FOB, but I'm not in command of anyone except for MT, uh, Spec Sutikal," the major said.

"Well, sir, it's good to see you're OK. We never thought they'd send you back to us here, though."

"You know the Big Suck, Corporal. It sends you where you're needed."

Aiden laughed out loud at that. He'd been around enough soldiers to hear the Army called "The Big Suck," but for an O to say it was unexpected.

Then he sobered up. Where the major was needed was back at the FOB because someone somewhere knew something about Corporal Aiden Kaas, USMC, one each.

"Uh, Major, I need to tell you something. I . . . I don't know where to start. But it has to do with why you're here. About me, that is."

The major visibly perked up. Aiden still harbored slight doubts about MAJ Ward, that the major had been playing him all along. Having his gut blasted open, though, was real dedication if that was true.

Aiden took a deep breath, then took the plunge. "Whoever told you about me was right. There's something about me that you should know. I'm a werewolf."

Chapter 34

Keenan stared at Kaas in shock. There, it was confirmed. He never really believed it, despite the colonel's insistence. And now, deep in the frigging Hindu Kush, Kaas admitted it.

"No shit," he said quietly, but his heart was racing.

"I know you don't believe me—"

"No, son, I believe you. That's what was suspected, but until now, until you told me, I thought I was on a wild goose chase—we were on a wild goose chase."

"You knew? Others know? How much does everyone know?" Kaas asked, his voice rising in what could be panic.

"Not much, Corporal. There have been suspicions, and then when your blood was tested—"

"They took my blood? When?"

"At Fallujah, when you were wounded. I actually looked into your case when you killed those three Al Qaeda in hand-to-hand, but your records were that you'd been sick, and according to our information, uh . . . *werewolves* . . . don't get sick."

"Oh, about that, I was sick before, when I wasn't one, when I was human—not that I'm not human now," he added hurriedly. "Then I was bit, and when I got sick, that was the seed fighting my T cells, and—"

"Slow down, son. 'Seed?' 'T cells?' Can you back up and tell me what happened?"

"Sure, sir. And you need to know, 'cause I kind of did something when you were WIA."

The young man was obviously agitated, which Keenan put down to his reluctance to give information. But he started with being bit, back at Fallujah, by a *varg*, how the varg's seed started a transformation in him, how he became a varg with the help of another, this one a *blood*, or someone born a werewolf. Kaas was a *kreuzung*, someone who had been transformed into a werewolf. Keenan wanted to ask more questions about that, but Kaas was on a roll and he didn't want to interrupt the corporal. All of this was fascinating, and despite his initial dismissal of the existence of werewolves, he was eagerly digesting everything Kaas was saying as the corporal veered from one train of thought to the other.

Evidently, the first shift to a werewolf—*fucking A, I'm sitting here quietly accepting that they even exist as if nothing was weird about it*—was quite difficult, and the local werewolf had helped him. From there, like a newborn, he had to practice to become better at shifting.

Kaas went over some of the fights he'd gotten into, including the one outside of Ramadi that had caught his attention again, the one that had ended up exposing Kaas' blood to the colonel's testing. Even as a werewolf, that sounded like a serious fight, and the Apache that took out a couple of the Al Qaeda could just as easily have taken Kaas out, he thought. An Apache could take out a tank, so he doubted a werewolf could stand up to one.

The narrative shifted to Afghanistan, and when Kaas explained about the air strike that Keenan had authorized, that opened up an entirely new field of questions. There were werewolf villages out there? And others attacking them? Keenan hoped he'd been on the right side with the air strike, but that could wait for later.

Finally, Kaas' story got up to where Keenan was hurt. The corporal was getting visibly agitated, which struck Keenan as odd. The Marine hadn't been hurt; Keenan had. Keenan still wasn't sure why he'd been targeted, but his suspicions kept reaching back to the Pentagon. It didn't feel right for having been a green-on-blue attack.

"You were so fucked up, sir, and Doc, he said you weren't going to make it, so I, well, I kind of bit my tongue, and then I spit my blood into your stomach," he said in a rush, anxious to get it all out.

What the fuck? He what?

"You spit your blood onto my wounds?" Keenan asked, flabbergasted.

"I'm sorry, sir. I just thought you were gonna die, and well, we can heal most things, and I hoped maybe my blood could help you. I thought it was your last chance."

"So, you spit blood *inside of me?*" he asked, looking down at his belly as if he could see inside the mostly healed wounds. "What possessed . . . uh, is that normal for you, uh, people?"

"I don't know," the corporal said miserably. "I just don't know. Hozan said it couldn't have made any difference. But maybe he's wrong, you know? You were really fucked up. Ask Doc. But when you got to the aid station, it wasn't so bad."

Keenan got the feeling that Kaas was grasping at straws. And there was something else there that Kaas wasn't saying. Keenan wondered what it could be when it suddenly hit him.

"You put your blood into me? And that should be more effective than just like a bite, like what happened to you. So now, you're going to be my patron? I'm going to be one of you?" he asked, excitement building despite himself.

Keenan had never felt stronger, despite having his gut blown open. He put that down to drugs, lots of drugs, but was there something more to it? The more he thought about it, the more he was sure he was right.

If anything, Kaas seemed more miserable than ever as Keenan said that. Keenan didn't understand why unless maybe there were werewolf rules on who was able to join them.

"Is that it?" Keenan asked. "Am I right?"

"Sir, that's the thing. I told you I'm a kreuzung, right? I'm not a blood. Only a blood can transform someone."

Keenan felt his heart fall. He wasn't sure why he was so disappointed. It had only been a flash of excitement, nothing he'd expected, yet he somehow felt that something had been yanked away from him.

"So, no werewolf for me," he said, trying to make light of it. "Your blood might have helped me, so it's sort of like a transfusion. Nothing weird. And if it helped, great. Now, it's back to normal."

"Uh, not really, sir," Kaas said.

Something in the corporal's voice grabbed Keenan's full and undivided attention.

"What do you mean?" he asked not sure he wanted to hear the answer.

"I have the seed, sir, like any of the Tribe. It wants to transform you, and it's going to try. But, sir, it's like this. My blood, the part that makes me different, well, it's like a copy of that in a real blood. It works for me, but it's a little off. A blood's seed is pure—mine is not. And it's not pure enough, I guess you could say, to win a fight with the T cells. Your T cells are gonna win."

"So, my immune system wins. No biggie. It wins against the flu, too."

"You don't understand, sir. When the seed gets destroyed, it sort of self-destructs."

"And . . . ?" Keenan asked, now positive he didn't want to hear the answer.

"And it poisons the body. You can't survive it.

"I've killed you, sir!"

Chapter 35

It was only a few hours later that MAJ Ward first complained of a headache and then before he could make it to the aid station, collapsed. Aiden heard about it and rushed to the aid station only moments after the major had been carried in. The medic attending the major was about to shoo him away, but MAJ Ward saw him and asked for him to be allowed to stay.

The medic looked at Aiden with disapproval radiating from his eyes, but he nodded and pointed to a small folding stool near the head of the gurney on which the major lay, an IV already pouring fluids into his arm.

The doctor came up looked at the major's chart, then told him it was probably an infection resulting from his recent wounding and surgery. He ordered a full range of antibiotics and told the medic he wanted the major monitored closely. If his fever didn't come down, he wanted the major to be put in an ice bath.

"Is this it?" the major quietly asked Aiden after the doctor left.

"Maybe, sir. I don't know, though. I was out when it hit me, and you're conscious, so maybe the doctor's right. Maybe it is from your injury."

The major leaned his head back on his pillow. "I don't think so. I can almost feel my body coming apart. How long do I have?"

"Hozan, he's the one I told you about, he says one or two days."

"Well, fuck," the major said when he heard that before falling quiet.

If Aiden thought the major was giving up, his next words dispelled it.

"Your Hozan is wrong. You survived, and so will I," he said with conviction.

Specialist Sutikal arrived, still in PT gear, his blade prosthetic gleaming in the aid station's lights. He glared at Aiden as if he blamed him for the major's condition. Aiden wondered if and how much the major might have told his assistant about him.

A nurse and a medic came up, ready to administer the doctor's orders, so Aiden quickly told the major he'd be back. He slipped out of the aid station, then went to the DFAC to find Hozan. He found his friend in the pot shack, as usual.

"It's started," Hozan said before Aiden could say anything.

"Yes. Major Ward's in sickbay now. He's got a fever."

"It is only a matter of time, now. It will be over soon," Hozan said in a calm voice.

"Uh . . . can you . . . I mean, I've been thinking. What if, you know, what if you bit the major? I mean, you're a blood, so your seed could transform him, couldn't it?"

Hozan stopped scrubbing the pot in his hand and seemed to consider it for a few moments. After a few moments more, he shook his head and went back to cleaning.

"No."

"What do you mean, 'no!' Why not?" Aiden asked, grabbing Hozan by the shoulder and spinning his friend around to face him.

Hozan seemed to bristle, and for a moment, Aiden thought he was going to shift. Hozan took a deep breath and slowly reached up to grasp Aiden's wrist and pulled Aiden's hand off his shoulder.

"First, it is forbidden. It takes Council approval to transform a human," he said, holding up a hand to cut off Aiden's protest.

"Second," he continued, "it just isn't done. I've never heard of two of us infecting the same human. If we could, it would have been tried before.

"Third, it is too late. It would take my seed a week or more to gain the strength needed to start a transformation, and by then, your major would be dead. I'm sorry, Aiden, but it won't work. You have to accept facts."

Aiden wanted to argue. He didn't give a flying fuck about the Council. No one gave any permission for him to be turned. But the logic on the timeline sunk in. He had to accept that.

Without another word, he turned and left to go back to the aid station. At least he could give moral support.

"Hey, how is he?" Cree called out as Aiden walked by oblivious to those around him.

"Oh, not good," he replied. "The doctor says it's an infection from where he was blown up. I'm going back to check on him."

"Look. We give you shit about the major, and we still don't know what's up between you two, but the guy's righteous, and it ain't right that he's fucked up after all that's happened. Some of the guys, well, we're going to stop by in a few, OK?"

Aiden was surprised at the offer—and touched. His team, his family here in Afghanistan, was there for him. "Sure, that would be great."

"Take it easy, bro. See you in a few."

Aiden walked back to the aid station and up to where they had the major. MAJ Ward was no longer conscious.

"He went out a few minutes after you left. He said something, like not blaming you?" Spec Sutikal said as Aiden came alongside the bed. "What did he mean?"

"Don't rightly know. He did tell me that he was here to watch me," he said, sure that Sutikal at least knew that much. "Stupid goose chase, if you ask me," he added.

With that, Aiden took a seat on the small stool, knowing he was doing no good, but wanting to be there anyway. Cree, Manny, and Doc found him there fifteen minutes later. The three took over the empty bed next to the major's, quietly chatting about inconsequential banalities. It wasn't important what they were saying, only that they were there.

When the major went into seizures, everyone jumped up and got out of the way of the medics and nurses. Within a few minutes, the seizures stopped, and the medical staff cautiously stepped back.

"Get Doctor Hildago," one of the nurses told a medic.

Aiden watched the major, almost expecting the man's breathing to stop when he felt eyes upon him. He looked up, and as the medic pushed open the doors to go get the doctor, Aiden saw the ANA lieutenant, the one Hozan said was some sort of hunter, standing there, looking in.

"Hey, Cree, do me a favor, OK?" he asked, turning away from the Afghan.

"Sure, bro. What?"

"That fucking ANA lieutenant out there, he's just staring at us. And you know, someone tried to kill the major. I'm getting a bad vibe about him."

Cree looked up, then without saying anything else, stood and strode to the door, Doc following him. He pushed it open and confronted the lieutenant, Doc at his side. The medical staff craned their necks for a moment to see what was going on and then looked back at their patient, leaving whatever grunts wanted to do to the grunts.

The ANA lieutenant looked back in through the open door at the major, then wheeled and walked away. Cree and Doc came back and sat down.

"I bet it was that fucker," Cree said. "I don't trust any ANA, but especially him."

Just then, the major went into another seizure. Aiden jumped up and helped the staff hold him down, waiting for the doctor to return.

What is keeping the guy? Aiden wondered, fearful of the major's rigid, writhing body, but more fearful that it might stop. With the seizure, at least Aiden knew he was still alive.

When the doctor finally arrived, he was quick. He ordered the waiting CASEVAC bird to turn rotors. He wanted the major back at the brigade aid station. Within ten minutes, the major was being taken out to the Black Hawk.

Aiden followed, stopping at the edge of the helo pad. He watched the major being loaded, and then the helo lifted off. Within seconds, the bird was lost in the darkness. The major was gone.

Chapter 36

Lomri Baridman Gorbat Wafa Khan eased back in the shadows. The American base was more open than a mountain village, and that didn't suit him, but he would have to make do.

The scene at the American hospital troubled him. Something had been off there and had sent his senses tingling. He was sure he'd been looking at a *wargalewa*, but with so many men there, which one was it?

The fact that the *wargalewa* was American gave him only the slightest pause. His ancestral duty transcended all else. Allies or not, the spawn had to be eliminated. He knew he might have to disappear once the job was done. The Americans had long memories, and they would not stand for one of their own being killed, even if they knew what it was that wore their uniform.

After being chased out, Gorbat waited outside the hospital, trying to open his senses. The longer he waited, the more confident he was that a *wargalewa* was inside. After fruitless years, he was finally going to get his chance to prove himself.

When they brought the American *jagraan*[45] out and loaded the wounded man on the helicopter, Gorbat stared at each of the figures, looking for clues. He didn't think it was one of the medical soldiers. A *wargalewa* would not be helping others. No, it had to be one of the fighters. These fighters were *Marines*, he had found out. He didn't know the difference between Marines and American Army soldiers, but some of his men had told fanciful tales of how fierce and cruel they were. Yes, a *wargalewa* would gravitate to such kind.

The Americans watched the helicopter lift off before breaking up and wandering off to wherever they were going. The one who took most of Gorbat's attention, the one he thought might be the

---

[45] Jagraan: Major

creature, split from the rest and disappeared between the plywood buildings 20 meters from where Gorbat stood in the darkness.

This was his chance!

Giving praise to Allah for his luck, he hurried across the open area around the landing pad and ducked down the same path as his target. His pulse raced with excitement. He was honest enough to know there was a bit of fear there as well. That did not bother him. Any sane man would fear these things. It was how a man confronted his fear that determined his status. Gorbat would not falter.

For a moment, he could not see anything and wondered if it had known he was on its trail and was lying in wait. But no, up ahead, it was walking confidently.

Gorbat reached into the small pouch he carried around his neck and pulled out the wide silver ring that was an essential part of any *shkaarzan's* tools. It gleamed in the moonlight as he slipped it on. Gorbat could see the ancient inscriptions, put on the ring before the time of the Prophet, but they were imbedded in his mind. He didn't know their meaning, but he could picture each curve and angle of the inscriptions in his mind.

He hurried forward, closing the distance. He focused on remaining silent. Surprise was a must. The creature was whistling, which was to its detriment. The sound helped mask Gorbat's approach.

He closed his left hand on his *pesh-kabz*, readying it for the strike. He would rather use his clean hand for that, but his ring had to be on that hand for it to have its full effect. No matter. He'd practiced often enough with his left to still be quite deadly with it.

He came up behind the creature, looking for bare skin. Not much was exposed. Making his decision quickly, he reached out with his right hand and took the thing by the wrist, pulling it around as he brought up his *pesh-kabz* to be ready for the killing blow.

"*Watthefukudooin?*" the American said. "*Eyelfukinkillyoo,*" he added, pulling his M4 up at the ready.

Gorbat immediately pushed the *pesh-kabz* into its sheath. This was not the creature. His silver ring had no effect on the man. Yes, he had the single eyebrow that could be a sign of a *wargalewa,* but some humans had that, too. He'd been aggressive back at the hospital, and he'd had the sign, but he was human.

Gorbat didn't understand what the American was shouting. He knew was "fuk" meant, something his men had adopted, but the tone of the man more than conveyed his anger.

"*Sorry*," Gorbat said in his broken English. "*Where food?*"

"*Shit*," the man said, using another word his men had quickly adopted. "*Yoorgonnagityurselfkild*," he added, but pointed back to where the dining hall was located.

Gorbat gave a half-nod, then stepped back. He had come close to killing the man, but even if the Americans were not his people, Gorbat was not a murderer. He would kill, but only when justified.

Somewhere in this camp, a *wargalewa* roamed, and he was going to kill it.

Chapter 37

Nikolai got out of the BMW, ignoring Akram, who he'd brought along as his driver. Well, bodyguard, too, not that one bodyguard would make much difference if the Council wanted him out of the way. Unfortunately, he couldn't bring Akram with him into the small, unobtrusive house that served as a club for some of the Council members. Nikolai had to go inside with an air of someone in power, someone unafraid.

Nikolai took in a deep breath of air, playing the scents in his nose. He hated coming to Germany, which was why he avoided most Council business. Langerich was supposedly in the country, but even to his human nose, it stank of machines and hopelessness. Why the Council insisted on having its headquarters in the middle of a human industrial cesspool was beyond him.

Nikolai subconsciously pulled down on the back of his western jacket as he entered the club. He could feel his pulse rising. Nikolai had been an alpha for over 40 years, and he'd faced many threats over that period of time, but deep inside, he knew what he faced now was far more serious than anything else he'd overcome.

It was foolish to think that his failed attack could escape notice. It was bad enough that he moved against other lycans without authorization, even if they were ferals. But to have his force wiped out by humans raised a hue and cry that bordered on panic.

Bee kwato, he thought, borrowing the Pashto phrase for someone with no balls.

Yet he also knew that those cowards would happily take off his head if they thought it would make their soft lives any safer. He was ashamed that this is what his kind had come to, to have such worms in charge of their once powerful tribe.

Nikolai puffed out his chest and strode in, trying to portray someone without a care in the world, someone sure of himself. He hoped the stink of stress was not emanating from him. He immediately caught site of Günter Wais, sitting in an overstuffed chair, sipping on what had to be a single malt. It was Günter who had first approached him while he waited to be called before the Council to give his version of the events in Afghanistan. Günter had been one of Nikolai's supporters when he asked for the go-ahead to attack the village, so Günter's request was not too surprising. Nikolai was not attuned to the politics of the Council, a result of his ignoring it over the years, so any possible lifeline thrown his way had to be taken—after first assuring himself that the lifeline was not really a noose.

Günter motioned for Nikolai to take the seat next to him. He sank into the chair, for once, happily taking in the deep, earthy smell of ancient, but well-cared-for leather. A glass of a single malt was on the small table beside the chair, and Günter motioned for Nikolai to take it.

The heady, complex notes of the whiskey swirled in his nose, and he had to restrain himself from shifting so he could explore every nuance. Shifting in this club, however, was not quite *verboten*, but close to it. Shifting could be a signal for an attack, so members kept in their human forms.

"So, Nikolai, it seems you fucked up pretty badly," Günter said as he looked over his glass at him.

Nikolai bristled at the comment, but he remained silent. Günter was one of the more powerful members of the Council, one who might be seeking the Prime Alpha position, if rumor had it right. Nikolai hated to take crap from another, but he needed to see where Günter stood and how that might affect him.

"I had . . . a setback," he responded non-committedly.

Günter let out a low, throaty chuckle and said, "Yes, I guess you could call it that."

"We were surprised when the humans attacked with aircraft, so we withdrew before we could be exposed," Nikolai said, wondering how much the Council knew about what had happened.

"'Before you were exposed?' I would say losing almost all of your force was rather after-the-fact for that."

Hozan held his gaze steady as his mind reeled. Evidently, the Council was completely aware of how many had been killed.

"So, Nikolai, what do you intend to do about it? The Council will want to know tomorrow, and I am curious as to what you are going to say."

"The feral tribe must be wiped out. They are a threat."

"I don't know, Nikolai. It seems to me that your bungling is more of a threat than some quiet little tribe hiding high up in the mountains."

Nikolai stood up at that, hands clenching in anger. Günter merely sat in his seat, completely relaxed. After a moment, he flipped over one hand, pointing back at Nikolai's chair. The fact that he was so at ease had an effect on Nikolai. He did not want to be submissive to anyone, but Günter reeked of Alpha. He sat back down and tried to regain his composure.

"Do you want a chance to get back at those who hurt you? I'm not talking about that primitive village, but the Americans, the military who conducted the attack?"

Despite himself, Nikolai felt a surge. What did Günter know? Nikolai hadn't even concerned himself if it was the Americans, Russians, or whoever who had conducted the airstrike. Did Günter know of the second attack, on the Afghan village, the one where two more of his tribe got killed, including his own sister's son?

"Would you be surprised to know that there is a *kreuzung* bastard, an unauthorized transformation, who is with the American military who attacked you?"

"I would be very surprised, Günter. But what does that have to do with me? It was the air forces that attacked us, not a lycan."

"If that feral bastard led the attack, would that interest you?"

"Yes, it would," Nikolai answered in complete honesty.

"This abomination should have been put down long ago, but he is the bastard seed of Nemir Muhmood's son. Omar was about as warped as they come, a mad dog whose death was welcomed by many, but Nemir won't let the order be given to remove his get. He's pulled in favors to block any action, the correct action, I might add, due to his idiotic affection for his son's only seed."

Ah, it is slowly becoming clear, Nikolai thought, sensing a way out for him.

"Now, if you were to take care of this troublesome problem, I think I can gather enough support to subvert any action that might be taken against you. A favor deserves a favor, right?"

He does want to be Alpha Prime, Nikolai realized. And this can help me.

Technically, all Günter had to do was to challenge Mario Suarez, the current Alpha Prime. But without support of the rest of the Council, or at least a majority of it, his reign would be short-lived as lycan after lycan challenged him until he was killed. Nikolai knew that Nemir Muhmood was closely aligned with the Prime. If there was a conflict between the two other Council members, then weakening Nemir could only help Günter. Implied in Günter's offer was that Nikolai would be in his camp when the time came.

Nikolai didn't give a rat's ass who was Prime. He wouldn't be here now if he hadn't been summoned. But if Günter would make sure that Nikolai left Langerich with his head intact, then that was an easy deal to make.

Günter made him uncomfortable. He knew that Günter's "alphaness" was greater than his own, and he had to fight to push down the submissiveness that kept trying to surface. This was a feeling that both disgusted and frightened him. However, the pragmatic side of him knew that if he were valuable to Günter, then he would be safe.

He didn't buy the fact that this unauthorized *kreuzung* had anything to do with the attack on his people. He knew that Günter was just trying to manipulate him. But if that was the price to pay for Günter's support, then it was an easy price, one that he'd have no qualms paying.

"I think you are right. A favor *does* deserve a favor, and I would be more than happy to take care of your *kreuzung* for you."

Chapter 38

Keenan opened his eyes and stretched. It was going to be a good day, he knew, and he felt up to whatever was thrown at him.

Wait! What the hell? he wondered, sitting up.

He looked around, confused. He certainly wasn't back at the FOB. He was in a modern, well-equipped hospital.

"Hey, where am I?" he asked a short woman in blue scrubs who was walking by.

"Welcome back to the living, Major. You're at SSG Heathe Craig Joint Theater Hospital," she said, turning to step up beside his bed.

"You mean at Bagram?[46]" he asked, still confused.

"That's right, Major," she said.

"Uh, how did I get here? What's going on?"

"You gave us quite a scare, Major. You were CASEVAC'd here three days ago. I don't mind telling you we didn't think you were going to make it. You spiked at 108, and people just don't come back from that. But Dr. Timmons took your case, and he was pretty aggressive, and, well, you're here, looking at a full recovery. Now that you're awake, I know Dr. Timmons is going to want to see you, so if you're feeling up to it, why don't I go get him, OK?"

"Uh, well, yeah, I feel pretty good, actually," he said as he realized he really did feel good. Better than good.

He lay back down while the nurse hurried off as he tried to wrap his head around what had happened. The last thing he remembered was being at the FOB aid station, sick with a fever. Kaas had come by and confirmed that this was the werewolf thing, the one that was supposed to kill him. He hadn't bought into it. He'd been determined to fight it, but when the fever had hit so quickly, along with nausea and trembling, he'd been scared, pure

---

[46] Bagram: the largest Coalition military facility in Afghanistan. It is located about 25 miles north of Kabul.

and simple. He remembered Kaas rushing out, then asking for something cold to drink. Then he remembered waking up here.

Does that mean I'm not going to die? he wondered. *Have I beaten it?*

Does that mean I'm one of them now? he asked himself as his train of thought went in the most logical direction.

He looked down at his left hand. There was an IV shunt still sticking into the back of it. Other than that, it still looked like his hand. It wasn't covered in hair or tipped with claws. He didn't *feel* like a werewolf, not that he knew what being a werewolf felt like.

Within a few minutes, the doctor arrived, trailed by two others. He picked up the chart at the end of Keenan's bed, something Keenan thought was ingrained in every doctor's DNA while at medical school. He glanced at it for only a moment before coming around and introducing himself.

"Dr. Timmons, Major. It's a pleasure to meet you, a real pleasure," he said, leaning forward and using his fingers to open Keenan's eyes wider so he could get a better view of his pupils, Keenan guessed.

The doctor had a small Army lieutenant colonel's patch sewn to his scrubs, which was odd. In Keenan's experience, most Army doctors preferred the simple "doctor" to any rank.

"I guess I have to thank you, sir," he said before the doctor motioned him to open his mouth.

After a quick look, the doctor stood back up. "Frankly, you were pretty far gone, there, young man. Another 20 or 30 minutes and you would have been in a body bag."

Nice bedside manner, Keenan thought.

"But we got you into an ice bath, and started intravenous hydration and gastric lavage right there. I immediately suspected a massive infection from your previous injuries, but frankly, the cause was not important. We needed to cool you down, and you just weren't cooperating. It wasn't until we started hemodialysis that your temperature started to edge down."

"Hemodialysis?"

"Yes. We took your blood out, cooled it, and sent it back in a constant loop. Not many hospitals stateside can do that, but here young man, that saved your life. It was still touch-and-go, though. It took over a day for you to get back to 103 and another day to get to normal. Frankly, I thought we'd saved a vegetable. Your brain function was erratic. Given how long your body had been at such extreme temperatures, it was amazing that there was *any* function at all."

There he goes with that nice bedside manner.

"But you seem to have made a full recovery. More than that, there is no sign of the infection that caused the fever. We've sent your blood samples back to USAMRIID, but frankly, I don't expect to get back anything surprising.

Keenan knew about USAMRIID, the US Army Medical Research Institute of Infectious Diseases at Ft Detrick. He'd sent quite a few blood samples there himself.

"We're going to keep you here for a few days. I don't want a relapse. Then you're going home, Major."

"I feel pretty good, sir. I think I'd like to stay until the end of my tour," Keenan told him.

"Not going to happen, Major. Frankly, that's what got you in trouble in the first place. You suffered a serious injury, and you should have been sent home. Sending you back to your FOB was almost a death sentence, and frankly, if you hadn't made it here in time for us to do what we do, you would be dead now. No, you are going back, no matter what your command wants."

"My command got involved?"

"They've been monitoring your progress quite closely. When I announced that you were out of immediate danger, we received a message that you were to go back to your FOB. I wasn't having that, though. You've got some heavy hitters wanting you to go back, but I have my own. And frankly, with regards to medical issues, the Chief of Army Medicine outranks even a four-star."

A four-star? A four-star got involved?

"So you, my friend, are going home. You'll be stateside in three days, I would think.

"Anyway, it was a pleasure to meet you while you were conscious, Major. I'll be back to check on you, but duty calls," he said, holding out his hand and shaking Keenan's.

"*Frankly*, thank you," Keenan said quietly as Doctor Timmons left.

That got a chuckle from the nurse, who hadn't left yet. "Yes, 'Dr. Frankly,'" she said. "He's got a few idiosyncrasies, but he's sharp, and he really did save your life."

"I didn't mean anything derogatory. I'm grateful to him, all of you. I'm lucky to be alive, I know."

"No offense taken, Major. But now, *frankly*, duty calls for me, too. You've been pumped full of saline, but we need you to get some liquids into your stomach. You up for some clear soup?"

Keenan realized he was famished. "I'd like a lot more than soup, if you would. Like a nice big steak?"

"Take it easy, Major," she said with a laugh. "Let's start with the soup and then see how that goes down. Hold on, and I'll get it ordered.

Keenan watched her walk off, noticing the sway of her butt. He'd been at death's door, but here he was wanting steak and feeling a physical attraction to a woman. He felt great.

Maybe he really was a werewolf now. It was hard to accept, but something was going on with him. It could be simple euphoria at having cheated death, but something told him it was something far more drastic—and amazing.

He needed to talk with Kaas.

Chapter 39

Aiden slipped off to his meeting point with Hozan, ready for a last trip to the village. The team received surprising orders to retrograde back to the US immediately. There was quite a bit of speculation as to why they were going back, but something had to be up. They had spent the last two days preparing, and they were leaving the next afternoon. This would be Aiden's last chance to see his "tribe," as he had begun to consider them. But there was something else he needed to tell Hozan, something surprising, but welcome.

"Major Ward, he survived," he told Hozan as he came up to his friend.

For once, Hozan seemed at a loss for words. It took him a moment, but he managed to get out, "What? The sickness has passed?"

"Yep! I just got word. Spec Sutikal, his assistant, looked me up an hour ago and told me. He's completely recovered and heading back to the US," he said excitedly.

"I . . . that's impossible. No one survives the transformation when it's a kreuzung who bit him. Everyone knows that."

"Well, in this case, 'everyone' is wrong. He's free and clear. And *I'm* his patron!" he exclaimed, holding his hand up for a high-five.

"This is unheard of," Hozan said, ignoring the proffered hand. "I should let the Council know."

"Uh, about that," Aiden said, lowering his hand. "Well, you know, your vaunted Council isn't too sure about me, so if you tell them about the major, I don't know what they'll do. Maybe we can keep this on the down-low?"

"The 'down-low?'" Hozan asked.

Aiden sometimes forgot that Hozan was still learning English. The ability lycans had to learn languages was good, but that didn't mean they could pull definitions for new words or phrases out of the thin air.

Insufficient.

"A secret. Not tell anyone."

Hozan considered this for a moment and then said, "Of course. You are right. This should be on the down-low for now, at least until we can understand this. I am pleased that your major survived, but I have to wonder if he's been turned. He may never have the ability to shift. That has happened before to some. They survived the sickness, but were forever human. If your major is like this, if he can never shift, perhaps it is best if this is never mentioned."

"Oh, he'll shift. He's a tough son of a bitch. I just have to be there to help him," Aiden said confidently.

"We'd better get a move on, though. I've got reveille at zero-five-thirty, and I want to spend as much time at the village as possible. This could be the last time I see any of them."

Within moments, Hozan shifted and said in his guttural varg voice, "What are you waiting for, cub?"

"Eat me," Aiden said, stripping off his utilities.

He triggered the shift, as always savoring the flood of smells that assaulted his nose. He stretched, sensing the power of his muscles. Despite many attempts, he hadn't been able to make the full shift to a wolf. But even as a varg, he could understand the pull to stay in that body, to leave the human form behind.

He lunged forward, hitting Hozan high in the chest, knocking the older varg down.

"See if you can keep up, old man," he said over his shoulder as he vaulted the FOB fence and ran off into the dark.

Chapter 40

Gorbat was nodding off as he sat in a shadow on the roof he'd selected as his post. Beneath him, the shopkeeper whose building this was slept with his family, unaware that Gorbat had taken over his roof. It was a two-story building, and it offered both eyes on the American base as well as the road leading east out of the village and up higher into the mountains.

It was hard to keep awake, though, when he was on military duty all day. He had to remind himself of the importance of his holy mission. If he had to sneak off and catch a nap during the day, so be it. He wanted to be the best soldier he could, but his priority was as a *shkaarzan*.

It was still early in the evening, too early to be falling asleep. People were in their homes, but light peeking out from shuttered window openings attested that most of the villagers were still awake. He shook his head to clear it and settled in for a long night, just like the last few nights. The weather was still warm, at least, even if there was a hint in the night air of the coming winter that would soon blanket the mountains.

Despite his resolve to stay awake, he almost missed the dark shadow of something coming over the wall of the base. He wasn't quite sure what he saw, but his instincts screamed at him to draw his *pesh-kabz*. He stood up to get a better view, and as he did so, he caught sight of a shape darting to the shadows, a shape that resonated within the *shkaarzan* part of him.

Wargalewa!

As the creature started to run, Gorbat immediately realized that Allah must have chosen his position on the roof. The *wargalewa* would pass immediately below him. All Gorbat had to do was wait, then drop down with his *pesh-kabz* for the killing stroke.

He started toward the edge of the roof when another shape came over the base wall.

There were two of them!

That gave Gorbat pause. Taking on two of them was not a sure thing. It wasn't that Gorbat was afraid to die. He would sacrifice himself if necessary, but he didn't *want* to die, and even if he took out one of the creatures before falling, that meant the people of the village would be at risk from the second one, and there would be no *shkaarzan* left to protect them. Victory belonged to the bold, true, but acting rashly could have consequences. He needed a better plan if he was going to defeat two of *Shatyan*'s minions.

He stared down as one, then the other loped along the street leading to him. For a moment, he was reminded of two children at play, one chasing the other. He banished that thought. *wargalewas* did not "play." They were devoted to their master's plans. Whatever they were doing, it was evil, Gorbat knew. For a moment, he was tempted to initiate the attack, two of them or not. At least he could thwart some innocent paying the price tonight, even if it cost him his own life.

That impulse became moot, however, when the first creature darted into a side alley two houses down from where Gorbat was waiting. The second one followed the first, and Gorbat was left alone on the roof, watching and listening. A few moments later, there was movement in the trees at the edge of the village, then nothing. The creatures were gone.

Where are they going? he wondered. *Who will they prey upon?*

Gorbat knew there were numerous small villages in the mountains, villages without communications with the outside world. These would be fertile hunting grounds for the *wargalewas*. Gorbat said a little prayer for whatever village the things were headed to and swore to himself that he would eliminate this scourge before more innocents could suffer.

Chapter 41

Aiden got off the tram and turned left to get his luggage. Carousel 19 was quite a walk away, but he knew his mom would be waiting there for him. He had two weeks of post-deployment leave, of which he would spend the first four days in Vegas with his mom.

The team had returned to Lejeune, sure they had an immediate deployment somewhere to justify their quick departure from the 'Stan. To their happy surprise, nothing was up, and within three days, they were spread to the winds as they went on leave. Aiden was going to spend four days with his mom, then it was off to Hawaii to see Claire. She was going to try to get some time off, but even if she couldn't, they could spend evenings and the two weekends together.

As he approached the carousel, he spotted his mom sitting on one of the seats alongside the back wall. He broke into a jog, dropping his assault pack as his mom stood up and taking her in his arms. He gave her a hug, lifting her off her feet.

"Take it easy, Aiden!" she said with a laugh. "I'm getting too old for rough stuff!"

"You're as young as ever, Mom, and you know it!" he said, letting her back down. "It's good to be home."

"And I'm glad my Marine is back, safe and sound. Give your mother a kiss," she said, offering her cheek.

"Nice to see you, Aiden," a voice said from beside his mom as Aiden complied with the kiss.

He turned to see a young blonde woman standing up from where she had been sitting. Aiden hadn't even noticed her.

"Chloe?" he asked, wondering why she was there at the airport.

"Oh, you remember Chloe," his mom said. "The sister of Terri Brubaker, your date who got sick before prom?"

That wasn't quite how it had gone down. Terri Brubaker had played a nasty prank on Aiden, inviting him to take her to prom, and then laughing when he came to pick her up. Terri's real date and some friends had been there, as well as Chloe, but the mortified Aiden had only told his mother, who was waiting to drive them to the dance, that Terri had come down sick.

Aiden looked at Chloe, who didn't bat an eye. She had been there and knew the truth, but she didn't say anything to contradict his mother.

"Chloe's been a dear to me, especially after the, you know, the assault. She's been like a daughter to me, taking care of me. I keep telling her she's young, and she needs to be out having fun, but she says she likes being with me."

"Well, thank you, Chloe, for watching over my mom while I've been gone, but we're going to go home now."

Chloe had been a thorn in Aiden's side since he'd come back on his leave after Iraq. The young, under-aged girl had taken an interest in him when he'd shown up to woo, then drop Terri in revenge for her treatment of him, going so far as to offer herself to him, then sending him naked photos of her through the email. Aiden had pointedly avoided the girl, even after she sent him a message reminding him that she was now 18 and so legal.

She had developed into a very attractive woman, even better looking that Terri, but she was poison. Aiden wanted nothing to do with any of the Brubaker girls.

"Oh, Chloe drove me here, Honey, so of course she is coming with us," his mother said, missing the tension in the air.

Aiden chose to ignore Chloe as he took his mother by the hand and went to wait by the carousel. It didn't take long before his seabag came out, and the three went up the escalator and across the walkway to the parking garage. The walkway was covered, but the late-summer Nevada sun beat relentlessly down. It was brutal, but it was home.

His mother insisted that Aiden sit in the front while Chloe drove, and then proceeded to produce a litany of gossip and family news from the back seat, forcing Aiden to turn within his shoulder belt so he could face her. He was peripherally aware of the big hotels along the strip, including the new construction of the Center City complex. They got off the 15 at downtown and took Martin

Luther King up to North Vegas. Within ten minutes, they were pulling into the small rambler that was home. Aiden had sometimes been ashamed of their run-down home, but after serving in Afghanistan, it was a veritable palace.

They went inside and turned on the swamp cooler. It wasn't air conditioning, but it could lower the inside temperature pretty significantly. Aiden dumped his seabag on his bed, then came back out to where Chloe held out a cold Sam Adams for him. Aiden didn't trust her, but he wasn't going to turn down a cold beer.

"I'm going to change into shorts, so take a seat, Aiden, and then I'll be back and you can tell me all about your time out there. Chloe, you're going to stay for dinner, right?"

"Oh, no, Mrs. K," she protested. "This is Aiden's first night back. I'm sure you want him for yourself."

"Hogwash! You know you're always welcome, and Aiden needs someone his own age here. You're staying. I insist!"

"OK, Mrs. K, I'll stay," Chloe said.

"You didn't argue very hard," Aiden said as his mother went into her room.

"That's because I wanted to stay. I've only got you for four days, and I want to make use of all of them," she responded with a glint in her eye.

Aiden didn't know if that was a predatory glint or not.

"*You* don't have me at all. I am here for my mom. Then I am going to Hawaii to see my girlfriend. That's *girlfriend*, in case you missed it."

"Maybe. Maybe not. Look, I know I've been something of a bitch. And yes, I caught what you told your mom about prom. And I probably shouldn't have sent you those photos. I know another guy would have jumped on that. Jumped on me, I guess. But, I have to give you props. You held back, and while I was pissed then, now, I know that just goes to show what a good guy you are. The thing is, ever since you came back from Iraq that first time, I just can't get you out of my head. I even dream about you, if you can believe that. OK, I was too young then, but I'm not now. I just want you to give us a chance."

"Chloe, you're, well, you look great, but there is no 'us.' I've got a girlfriend, and, to be honest, I can't get past what you guys did to me. And yes, I saw you laugh."

"But then why did you come back and fuck Terri?" she asked, looking perplexed.

"No beating around the bush for you, I guess. I didn't mean to sleep with her. I wanted to impress her with my medals, then dump her, like she dumped me. But one thing led to another, and well, you know . . ."

"Yeah, I know. I've heard all about it. Terri says you were her best ever."

Aiden reddened at that, but part of him felt a surge of pride. *Her best ever?*

"She really wants you back, you know? But she's pregnant again, and this time she's keeping it," she said, a bit of the evil Chloe showing up in her voice.

"Pregnant? Again?"

"Yeah, like you know, she was preggers, but got an abortion. Now she's seven months, fat as a pig. She doesn't even know who's the baby daddy.

"Terri's fucked up her life, but that's not me. Maybe I was going the same way, but I'm not now. I'm even going to Pima to become a dental tech, you know, a real job."

Aiden didn't know what "Pima" was, but he didn't want to extend the conversation.

She reached out and put her hand on his forearm.

"Look, I know you don't like me. But you don't know me, either. Let me hang out with you, even here with your mom. I'm not as bad as you think, and I know I can make you happy. What do you say?"

Back in high school, Aiden couldn't get a girl to even talk to him. He would have given his left nut to have someone like Chloe come on to him. Now, since he'd been turned, he had Chloe, Terri, Kashmala back in the Afghan village, and Claire, all A-list girls, after him. He should have been happy, but it scared him more than anything else. He was scared most of all that Claire would come to her senses and realize him for the dweeb he really was. With the others, he was scared of himself, that he would give in to temptation.

Before he could answer Chloe, his mother came back out. "What are you two doing standing in the middle of the room? You don't need an invitation. Sit, you two," she told them indicating the couch while she took the chair.

"Did Chloe tell you she's in school now? She's going to become a dentist."

"Now Mrs. K, I told you I'll be a dental technician, not a dentist. But Aiden didn't come home just to hear about me," Chloe told her.

"Oh, you're right, what was I thinking?" she asked before turning back to Aiden. "Now, son, unless you're going to say it was all top secret stuff, how about telling us about Afghanistan. Was it exciting?"

Aiden dearly loved his mother, but her not-so-subtle attempt at a hook-up for him was frustrating. She knew he was with Claire. He decided to ignore it, though, just happy to be with her and seeing she looked none the worse after the break-in. He was going to give her—them—a very sanitized version of his tour, ignoring the combat—and, of course, that little werewolf thing going on.

He took a quick look at Chloe, who had scooted over until their legs were almost touching. It was going to be a long, long evening.

Chapter 42

Aiden's heart was pounding, his vision constricting as he wiped the sweat off of his palms and onto his shorts. He felt the pre-shift tremors flowing like electricity through his body, and he had to consciously keep from shifting right then and there.

He took a deep breath to calm himself, the salt air filling his senses. The sun had not set yet, and the sky was awash in color. The full moon was rising low on the horizon as if trying to drive off the sun. The evening was beautiful, he noted in the back of his mind. Surely, on such an evening, nothing could go wrong.

It was time—no more delaying it. He pulled the case out of his pocket and placed it on the sand.

"This is a volcanic beach," he called out to Claire, who was standing in a small tidal pool, bent over, looking at the tiny creatures for whom the pool was their universe. She wore a pink, flowered sarong which she had put on to cover her deep-purple bikini.

"I know. These islands are volcanic," she said, not looking up.

"You know what that means. There are diamonds all through this. I heard from the hotel staff that a tourist found a big one here this morning."

"Really?" Claire asked, standing up and looking around the beach. "No, I don't believe it."

"It's true. I bet you can find one if you try."

"Nah. If there ever was anything here, it would be ground to bits by now," she said, but she was looking interestedly at the sand beneath her feet.

"Wait a minute. Let me get my camcorder out," Aiden told her.

Aiden had bought a new Canon camcorder at the Nellis Exchange before flying out to see Claire. It was surprisingly small, and Claire had been a willing model for him earlier in the day up at Waimea Falls.

She struck a pose for him, hand on her hip, as he brought the camera up.

"Claire, like I told you, this is a video camera. I need action. Look for a diamond in the sand!"

"Really?" she said with a laugh. "OK. Here I am in Hawaii, prospecting for diamonds on the beach. Oh, here's one," she said, reaching down to pick up a small pebble. "Only 20 carats. Too small," she said, tossing the pebble over her shoulder.

"Keep looking. You're doing great," Aiden told her.

She played along, "finding" and then tossing various "diamonds." She was moving away from the small case he'd put down, though, and as the sun started to sink below the horizon, it was getting darker. Aiden tried to will her to turn around, but being a werewolf evidently didn't give him any mind control powers.

Finally, he had to break form, "How about in back of you? Turn around."

"Aiden, OK, isn't that enough?" she asked.

She complied, however, playing along. She took one step and bent down as if she found another one when the small case caught her eye.

"What's this?" she asked, taking two more steps and picking it up.

The sun was almost gone and the moon taking over when she opened the small case. A final ray of the sun reached across the ocean and struck the diamond, making it seem alive.

Aiden let the camcorder drop, held around his neck by the strap as he took several steps forward and knelt in front of Claire, all his anxiety culminating in a single burst of fear.

"Claire, I know we've been talking about it, but nothing's been formal-like. So, right now, here on the beach, I need to ask you. Will you marry me?"

She was quiet for a moment, turning the ring back and forth, catching the final rays of sunlight before the sun disappeared below the horizon.

Why isn't she saying anything?

She looked at Aiden and said "Yes!"

Aiden felt a wave of relief sweep over him. They had discussed a life together, sure, but he had always feared a change of heart on Claire's part. She was out of his class, but she didn't seem to realize that. And now, she was going to be his wife!

She flung her arms around his neck and pulled him up for a kiss: a very strong, passionate kiss. It was Aiden who had to break it to come up for air.

"I was wondering when you'd get up the nerve to ask me," she said, arms still around his neck, their faces just inches apart.

"I, uh, well, I was going to ask you—"

"Yes, before you deployed. But you didn't."

"You knew?"

"Of course I knew, Aiden. But my big hero Marine was too scared."

"Why didn't you say something?" he asked.

"Because some things need to be traditional. I'm a modern woman and a kick-ass Marine, but for some things, a girl's got to be asked," she told him. "And now that you've asked, you're mine, and there's no backing out. From here on, I'm taking over. I've already got my bridesmaids' outfits picked out, so until we say 'I do,' you're just along for the ride."

That was fine with Aiden. He wasn't much into weddings, so whatever she wanted was what she was going to get. He was just so relieved that she said yes that he'd agree to anything just to get their marriage signed, sealed, and delivered.

With his arms around her, his hands were resting on her butt. He became conscious of her bikini bottom under her sarong, and without thinking, he pulled her pelvis into his. She gave a little intake of air as she pulled tighter around his neck and returned the pressure to his crotch.

She looked around the beach, then said, "I want to pull you down on the sand and take you right here, to seal the deal, but we're not exactly alone, and it's still pretty light. What say you drag me back to the hotel and get these clothes off of me?" she asked.

Aiden didn't need her to say anything else. They had checked in to a small hotel on the western side of Oahu, somewhat off the beach, but a little higher in elevation so that it still had a view. It wasn't as nice as the Hale Koa, but it had a queen size bed, and that was what mattered now. He took Claire by the hand and led her over the sand and to the beach parking. He had to concentrate to obey the speed limit as he drove Claire's car to the hotel; something made more difficult both by his eagerness and by Claire's groping hand.

It was only a few minutes until he turned off the main road and made it to the hotel's gravel parking lot. It was dark already, but the full moon made up for the lack of street lights. From down the hill, a burst of laughter sounded from the local bar, but it was quiet at the hotel with only the trill of a gecko sounding out.

The hotel was set up as a series of bungalows, all probably built in the '50's. The trees and undergrowth had crept up around them, which gave the two the privacy they craved. They almost ran up the steps to the path that would lead them to Number 18, the last bungalow in the line.

Aiden was surprised when the three men stepped out from between two of the bungalows to block their way. He should have sensed them, but his senses had been more attuned to other, more prurient things at the moment. There was no mistaking the men's stances, however. They meant business.

"Hey, haole. How 'bout you give us your wallet, yeah?" one said, stepping forward.

The men looked to be local boys, both in clothing and accent, but something about them triggered the warrior in Aiden. He didn't know if it was the Marine in him or the werewolf, but he was certain that these were not three young men out to jack a tourist. They were professionals, he was sure.

He pulled Claire behind him and said, "Look, we don't want any trouble."

The leader looked back to the others and laughed. "Ai yah! He say he don't want no trouble. Well, maybe you betta give me your wallet, then," he added, turning back to face Aiden and Claire.

"We were just at the beach. I didn't take my wallet. I've got a twenty here with me, though. You're welcome to it."

"Twenty? You think we do dis for onna twenty? No way. What say we take you to your room, an den you give us any kine what we want."

"I know what I want," added one of the men in back of him. "I want me some haoli wahine. How 'bout it, sistah?"

Aiden felt Claire bristle as she tried to move around him. He held up his arm to stop her.

"Ooh! Look at dat, givin' me the stinkface! You bedda listen to your man, dere, girl. He trying to protect you."

The words were there. The language was there. But the more they talked, the more Aiden was sure these men were not casual muggers. The local pidgin seemed too forced. They were too alert, ready for action. But who were they? Had the Council finally decided to act? If these men were werewolves, then the two of them were in big trouble.

"Fuck you," Claire said, ready to fight.

Aiden felt a surge of pride for his fiancé. She was not a shrinking violet, that was for sure. But she had to keep in control.

"Oh, you like beef? I think it's time to kick your man's okole," the leader said. "You ready to give um, little man?"

If they were local thugs, then Aiden knew he had a chance. He might not be very big, and he was certainly much smaller than the three men in front of him, but he was stronger than he looked.

Still, he glanced behind him. All the bungalows were dark, but the hotel office wasn't too far away. Hopefully, the receptionist would hear something and call the police.

Looking back was almost his undoing. The leader rushed him and hit him low just as Aiden was turning back around. The man was strong—ungodly strong. He obviously knew what he was doing, too. This wasn't his first rodeo.

Aiden struggled to push the man off of him, and big hammer blows hit his face. It took two bucks, but he managed to throw the man off. His opponent rolled easily to his feet and stood balanced there, ready for Aiden.

The man was strong, but with a thrill, Aiden knew he was stronger. He could take him if the other two stayed out of it. If

Claire weren't there, he'd have shifted, but it was just possible that he'd be able to fight out of this as a human.

The man was ready for him, but he wasn't ready for Claire. No one was going to attack her man, and she flew into a superman punch, hitting the man from the side, sending him to his knees. Aiden took the opportunity to rush the man, sending one powerful punch to the guy's chin. Anyone else would have been knocked senseless, but the big man was only dazed. He glared blurrily at Aiden as he tried to regain his feet.

Aiden's blood was up, and he wanted to crush the man's skull. He moved forward, ignoring the others. Only Claire's scream cut through his single-mindedness. He looked around to see Claire, clutching her arm, blood seeping from between her fingers. The man who had said he wanted her was standing in front of her, casually holding a wicked-looking knife.

Whatever had been holding Aiden back disappeared in a flash of white rage. No one was going to get away with hurting Claire!

Within seconds, Aiden the human was no longer there. Aiden the varg appeared and let out a roar. The man with the knife stared up in shock at the sudden apparition that had appeared before him. He tried to raise his knife, but it did him no good. Aiden crashed into him, driving him to the ground. Aiden's jaws closed around the hapless man's throat, and with one jerk, the man was almost decapitated. Blood drenched Aiden, filling his mouth and covering his head.

The blood still spurted in an arc as Aiden vaulted over the body to where the third man had moved into some sort of martial arts stance. These were professionals, the human part of Aiden noted from somewhere in the back of his mind. That didn't matter. Aiden charged, taking the roundhouse kick off the side of his head as he crashed into the man. He put his arms around the man's torso, and looking right into the man's eyes, he squeezed. The anger in his opponent's eyes faded into panic, then as a loud snap filled the night, went cloudy. Aiden let go as the body slid limply to the ground.

Aiden turned to where the last man, the leader, had struggled to his feet. Aiden wondered if the man was armed, but even so, his time was about up. He moved forward, step by deliberate step, until he stood before the man.

"Who sent you?" he asked, the human words difficult for his varg body to make.

"Someone bigger than you," the man said, his pidgin accent gone. "And now I know why."

The flash of steel catching the moonlight was enough for Aiden. He moved his arm to block the man's knife, the blade burying itself in his forearm. Aiden reached with his other arm and grabbed the man's throat. There was no surrender, only hate in the man's eyes as Aiden squeezed the life out of him.

As he dropped the lifeless body to the ground, Aiden lifted his head and howled into the night. For a moment, the laughter and crowd noise still audible from the bar below went quiet, only to slowly pick up again in jerks and starts.

Aiden felt the familiar joy of victory, of proving himself against his enemies. Then he remembered.

He turned around to where Claire stood staring at him. She had let go of her arm, and now that arm was covered with blood, a stream dark brown in the moonlight as it flowed down her arm, onto her fingers, and dripped onto the ground. Her mouth was open as she tried to process what she had just seen.

Aiden shifted back. He was covered in blood, and his T-shirt was mangled, but at least he was human for the moment.

"Claire, it's me. Aiden!"

Chapter 43

Jack Tarniton leaned back in his chair, contemplating what he'd just seen. Part of him wanted to jump up and pump the air with his fist, but part of him knew it all along, so it really wasn't a surprise. It was good finally to get confirmation, though.

He was alone in a secured room on the third floor of the US Pacific Command headquarters at Camp Smith. In front of him was a monitor on which he'd just witnessed Aiden Kaas transform into a werewolf and kill the three men sent to trigger just such a reaction. The feed from a minicam on the team leader's shirt had been grainy, and the darkness affected the quality, but there was no getting around it. Kaas was a werewolf and a very effective fighting machine.

The men he'd sent, although they'd had orders not to kill Kaas for any reason and to try not to kill the girl, were some of the best operatives the country possessed. The colonel had smiled as he listened to the island lingo of the leader of the team. The man had been an all-American wrestler at Lehigh, then received a masters from Cornell, yet he had flowed into the part. The colonel regretted that the man was dead. He could have used someone like that for other operations. But sometimes, sacrifices had to be made.

Once Kaas' travel plans had become clear, the colonel had decided to avoid a confrontation in Vegas. Too many coincidences could spook the kid. So he'd gathered his troops and flown to Hawaii to oversee the operation himself. Ward was still recovering, although what to do with the major was still an issue, and Seagal was a limp-dicked civilian foisted on him. No, it had to be him, and he'd gotten results. There, on his laptop, he had the proof. Werewolves did exist.

What to do with the proof was still a question that he was pondering. He could report in with it, but he knew that he could then be shunted aside while his boss took the credit. At the Pentagon, a colonel was barely above the janitor who cleaned the latrines. But if he held onto it for now and developed it, then he might be able to make himself part of the program, someone too vital to push aside.

The colonel didn't see this as a way to cover his ass. He truly believed that he was the best person to run the program he envisioned, and *his* program would ensure the safety and viability of the country. It was not a self-serving intent, but a patriotic one.

He popped a thumb drive into his laptop, copied the recording, and pocketed the drive. The fact that he put classified material on an unclass drive meant nothing to him. The ends justified the means.

He finger only hesitated a moment before he hit the delete, erasing the recording from his laptop. He opened up an unauthorized program, one that guaranteed to completely eliminate all traces of a deleted program, past the efforts of the most skilled technician to recover it. With one click, the 0's and 1's started flooding the supposedly free memory of his hard drive. The program filled and deleted the memory seven times, and the recording was gone, truly gone.

The only proof that there was a werewolf in the United States Marine Corps was in his pocket as he left the building and walked out into the Hawaiian night.

Chapter 44

Aiden pulled the last body out of the trunk while Claire grabbed the slit-open garbage bags they'd used to line it. Two of the bodies had already been dumped in water past Makaha, and the third, that of the leader, was the last one. The body of the first man Aiden had killed had been the most mangled, the throat ripped open. The second man had a broken back, while the leader had been asphyxiated. Aiden didn't think the bodies would remain undiscovered, but hopefully, out on this desolate stretch of road, it would take awhile, and by then, the crabs would have made their impact on the bodies, and hopefully any DNA evidence linking Aiden and Claire to them would have been hopelessly corrupted.

They'd tried to clean up the mess the best they could, but Aiden had watched enough *CSI Las Vegas* to know that if the police got a hold of the car, they would find evidence of the three men. He just hoped it wouldn't come to that. Aiden had his clothes in another garbage bag, and he intended to burn them.

Even if the police never found the bodies, whoever sent them would know that they were missing. They would realize that the two of them were alive, and they would probably send more to finish the job.

What worried Aiden more was that Claire wasn't speaking to him. She dutifully helped clean up the mess. She went into the small local market for the garbage bags. She helped load the bodies into her trunk. But she hadn't said a word.

It wasn't every day that someone found out her fiancé was a werewolf, he knew, but he was hoping for some sort of dialogue. He needed to know what she felt.

Aiden had contemplated checking out of the hotel, but leaving at 11:00 p.m. was a warning flag, one that would be remembered if the police came around asking questions. So after dumping the bodies, they drove back. Claire took a shower closing the bathroom door. She came out and slid into the bed, ignoring him. Aiden looked at her for several moments, then sat down on the couch where he could look out the window. He stayed there all night, not sleeping, keeping watch.

In the morning, they cleaned up, gathered their bags, and checked out. Claire responded to questions with a few yeses and nos, but she didn't initiate anything. They decided—Aiden decided, that is, and she didn't object—to drive to the windward side of the island and find another cheap hotel for the night. Aiden would pay cash in case someone was tracking their credit card usage.

They drove back to Pearl City, then up the H2 past Schofield Barracks and the Dole pineapple plant. They had planned on touring the plant, but this didn't seem the right time to bring it up. When they reached Haleiwa, they stopped at a drive-in. Aiden was famished, as he usually was after a shift, and this time, after healing a knife wound to his arm, he was even hungrier. He took three teri beef plates. Claire raised her eyebrows as Aiden dug in, but her own appetite seemed strong as she took a loco moco plate and ate everything.

They drove back past Waimea Falls Park. It had only been yesterday there when things had seemed so bright to Aiden. Now, he had no idea what was happening between them.

They found a small, run-down surfer hotel. The big winter waves had not hit the islands yet, so they were able to get a room. Aiden paid cash, and the two walked into their refuge for the night.

"OK, Aiden, what the fuck?" Claire asked as soon as he locked the door.

Aiden felt a surge of relief. At least she was talking.

"I . . . uh . . . I'm sort of a werewolf," he got out.

"'Sort of?' It looked to me that was more than sort of!" she said. "And if you just asked me to marry you, don't you think you might have wanted to tell me about this?"

"I wanted to, but I was afraid that you'd, you know—"

"Afraid I'd walk out on you?"

"Yeah," he said miserably.

"I *should* walk out on you. You *lied* to me."

"I didn't lie. I just didn't tell you."

"Don't play games with me. I'm royally pissed at you, Aiden Kaas. Really, really pissed," she said, punching him hard in the shoulder. "You lied to me by not telling me."

"I know, Claire. I know. You've got ever right to be pissed."

"Damn right I do. And I should leave you. But I can't. Do you know why?"

Aiden shook his head.

"Because I love you, damn it all," she said, falling into him, arms around his neck.

Aiden tentatively put his arms around her and gently squeezed. They stood there, at the foot of the ratty bed, just holding each other. Finally, they broke apart, and Claire sat on the bed, patting beside her for Aiden to sit down.

"Look, I've had some time to think about it. I love you, and for the life of me, I'm not sure why. Don't take this wrong, but you're not really the kind of guy I'd date. My parents were amazed when I brought you home. You're not the most, well, handsome guy, the most A-list guy around.

"Oh, don't look hurt like that. You have to know that, too. But ever since you came up to me in the gym at Fallujah, well, there's something about you that pulled me in. I had no idea what it could be. And the more I knew you, the deeper I sank. You had something, something I could see that also attracted every other girl around. Now I know what it was. Vampires and werewolves, they have this thing, right? A supernatural thing. That was why I fell for you."

"But I'm still Aiden," he said.

"Yes, but evidently, this is part of Aiden, too. And I can't separate the two parts. I can't even believe I am sitting her rationally talking about werewolves, for goodness sake. But it is what it is. I love you, Aiden Kaas, and I want to marry you. But right here and now, we are going to sit until you tell me everything— everything. I need to know just what, I mean, who you are. If you can't, I'm walking right out of here, understand?

He did understand, and he felt as if a weight had been lifted from his shoulders. He had always wanted to tell her, but how do you go about telling the girl you love that you can change into a varg? Now, he had no choice.

He told her the entire story, from being born a "normal" human to being bit in Fallujah. He told her about his first shift, about his battles, about the changes in him. He told her about how the Council hadn't approved him being turned, and how he was on sort of a probationary status. This brought up questions on just what a werewolf was from a scientific standpoint, not fairy tales. When she found out about being infected with a bite, she perked up.

"So you mean, if you bit me, I would turn into one of you?" she asked.

"No, it doesn't work like that. I told you, I'm a *kreuzung*. I can't turn someone. Only a blood can."

He decided at that moment that he wouldn't go into any details about MAJ Ward for the time being.

"But if you did bite me, what would happen?"

"You would get sick in a couple of weeks, then die. Don't even think about it."

"Don't worry, I'm not ready to die yet," she said, but with what Aiden thought lacked conviction.

It took almost four hours to tell his story. Claire interrupted him continually with questions, which he patiently answered. The more they talked, the more at ease she seemed to become. It was almost as if the old Claire was back.

If anything, she seemed a little excited, so Aiden made sure to downplay what a werewolf was. He told her that while they were tough creatures, they could be killed. He'd taken one down with a silver knife, the one she'd bought him on Riverwalk, and that maybe a hundred had been killed during an air strike. Still, there was a sparkle in her eyes as she asked more questions. Finally, Aiden was talked out, his voice hoarse.

"I want to see you, in the light. Can you do that for me?" she asked.

Aiden wanted to say that she could already see him, but he knew what she meant. He was dreading this, but if he wanted her to trust him, to stay with him, this was inevitable. He stood up, took off his shirt, and stood there in his shorts. He faced her, then with a flip of his mind, shifted.

If she was shocked or horrified, she gave no indication. She looked at him, really looked at him, from the feet to his head. She stood, reached out, and ran a hand down his chest. She was simply feeling his pelt, he knew, but her touch sent shivers through his body. He strove to control himself. After several minutes, she seemed satisfied.

He shifted back and sat down. He tried to guess what she was thinking, if she could accept him.

She bent over and gave him a kiss on the forehead before going into the bathroom. She left the door open, and within a minute, he heard the shower turning on. He knew she wanted him to follow, but he sat on the bed, waiting.

Five minutes later, the water turned off. Aiden watched the door until Claire appeared, a towel wrapped around her. She sauntered, her hips swaying, until she was in front of him. With a flick of her wrist, the towel fell away.

"We never did consummate our engagement, Aiden. Now it's time."

And so they did.

Chapter 45

"I'm not sure, sir. I think it took me about three weeks, but it may not even happen to you. Hozan says there are cases like that," Aiden said on the phone from Claire's front room.

Claire had to work, so they had come back to her apartment on the K-Bay side of Oahu. She was still asleep, which gave Aiden the opportunity to take the call. MAJ Ward had gotten his number from his mother, and he was full of questions.

"Aiden, I told you I think it's about time we dropped the 'sir' thing. If you are my patron, then I think we are beyond the military formalities."

"Uh, right, sir, I mean Keenan," he said.

Some habits die hard.

"But with you, how did it happen? You told me this Hozan came after you turned into a werewolf the first time. Did you try to change, or did it just happen?"

"It just happened. I was hit in an ambush, and I think my body just tried to save me. I didn't try and change because I didn't know anything about it."

"Yeah, I forgot about that," the major—Keenan—said. "It just that, I feel weird, like a pupa in a cocoon, trying to get out. And it's been more than three weeks. My nerves are tight."

"I felt like that, too!" Aiden exclaimed. "For a week or so before I shifted that first time."

"Maybe I should just try and force it tonight," Keenan said.

"Uh, I wouldn't do that, sir. Like I told you, I might not have been able to shift back without Hozan there. It's not, well, it's not easy. Look, I'll be going back to Lejeune in a week. If you can get down there, let's get together. But don't try anything until then. Remember, all we know is that you survived the sickness. We don't know if you'll ever be able to shift."

"Who'll never be able to shift?" Claire said from her bedroom door.

"Oh, shit, sir, I need to go. I'll call you back," Aiden said, hanging up.

"What?" he asked stupidly.

"Who are you talking to?"

"Uh, nobody important."

"Look, Aiden, I told you we need to trust each other. You are talking to someone who's been infected, someone who survived the 'sickness,'" she said, making the quotation marks with her fingers. "I need to know who infected this person, this officer I'm guessing from how you're speaking to him. Tell me."

Aiden wrung his hands. He'd lied to her, the one thing she said was unacceptable. But she's seemed so excited, so intrigued, he hadn't wanted her to be tempted to become a werewolf. Even if the major had survived, Aiden was not willing to risk Claire like that.

As she looked expectantly at him, Aiden sensed this was a turning point. If he lied to her, she would be gone.

"That was Major Keenan Ward. He was sent to watch over me, to find out what I was. Someone tried to kill him in Afghanistan, and not knowing the consequences, I infected him, trying to save his life. I didn't know at the time that as a *kreuzung*, I was killing him."

"He didn't sound too dead to me, or can werewolves also talk with ghosts?" she asked dismissively.

"No, of course not. Somehow, on a million-to-one shot, he survived. I don't know how. And Hozan, he says the major probably won't ever be able to shift."

"I suppose it was Hozan who told you that this major would die, too?"

"Uh, yeah, it was him."

Claire stepped into the front room and took a seat next to Aiden on the couch. "Aiden, I love you dearly, but you are so fucking naïve at times. You told me about the conflict in this Council over you, and you told me that Hozan was sent to watch over you. Don't you think he would want to discourage you from bringing in yet another unsanctioned werewolf?"

"No, it's not like that. Hozan's my friend. I trust him."

"You trust too many people. You even said this major was sent to watch you, too. So at least two people were sent to watch you, and these are the people you trust?"

"Hozan helped me, and he still does. He's my friend."

"And why didn't you tell me before that you'd infected this major, and that he was still alive?"

"Because I didn't want you to be tempted. I can't bear the thought of losing you," he said, taking her hand in his.

"So because you love me, you lied to me," she pointed out.

"Yes, and I'm sorry, so sorry," he said, afraid of what she would say next.

"And maybe your friend lied to you, to protect you?"

"I . . ." he started before stopping and thinking over what she had just said.

"I don't think so," he finally said.

"If you could lie to me with all the best intentions, then Hozan could have lied to you. If the Council got word of what you had done, there could be pretty serious ramifications, from what you told me. Maybe it has already started. We still don't know who sent those men who attacked us."

If the Council had sent a death squad, Aiden was pretty sure it would have sent vargs. He didn't bring that up, though.

"Look, I've got to get to work. Go ahead and call back your major. We need to see if what Hozan said was right or if the major's now a full-fledged werewolf, too.

"I've got to shower and get into my uniform, but we've got some serious talking to do tonight," she told him in a brook-no-argument tone of voice as she stood and kissed his forehead.

Aiden's life was on a roller-coaster ride at the moment, and he had no idea when it would stop.

Chapter 46

Claire seemed in a good mood as they drove back from dinner. They had just gone to Roy's Waikiki for dinner, which was fabulous. Aiden's short ribs and Claire's duck breast were fantastic. The meal was not cheap, but it was about the best food Aiden had had in a long time.

The meal put them in a good mood, but still, this was Aiden's last night on the island, and he would have expected Claire to be a little sad about that. Her happiness disappointed Aiden in a way that he couldn't explain.

The week together had been good, but there had also been an undercurrent of strain. For two days, Claire had tried to convince Aiden to bite her, to turn her. She was sure that she was strong enough to survive the transformation, especially after browbeating Aiden enough for her to talk to the major on the phone.

Aiden didn't think the major was too happy about that, but screw it. If he was going to make anyone happy, it was Claire, not him. But he had spoken to Claire at length about his experiences, and after Claire had gotten off the phone, she had been ever more convinced that she could handle it.

But no pressure was going to change Aiden's mind. He was not going to risk her. The major had been lucky, and that had no bearing on Claire. Aiden refused, flat and simple.

They chatted about the future as he drove them back. Rather, Claire chatted, mostly about the wedding plans back in Texas. Her father insisted on having the wedding in San Antonio, and other than his mother, there was no one in Vegas he really wanted to invite. Aiden just listened, interjecting enough "uh-huhs" and "yeses" to show Claire he was listening.

His mind was wandering, however. During the major's last call, he had told Aiden that a patrol of 12 ANA soldiers and five US soldiers from the FOB had been ambushed. All seventeen men had been killed and "mutilated," the reports read. Both of them were concerned that the men hadn't been mutilated after death—that the damage had been done in the attack, and by vargs. The fact that it had happened to soldiers from FOB Ballenstein couldn't be a coincidence. Aiden wanted to speak with Hozan, but he wasn't sure how to contact him.

They pulled into the apartment complex, and with Claire chatting away, climbed the stairs to her second-floor unit. He plopped down on the couch as Claire opened the fridge and got out a Primo for him. Aiden rather liked Longboard better as far as Hawaiian beer went, but Claire liked Primo, so Primo it was.

"I need to use the head," she told him as he turned on the TV.

An episode of *COPS* was on, this one from Kansas City. He settled back to watch.

It took awhile, maybe 20 minutes, and *COPS* was almost over when the door to the bedroom opened, and Claire came out. Aiden almost choked on his beer. She was in a lilac barely-there negligee of some sort, one that left nothing to the imagination. With the confidence of a lioness on the hunt, she glided across the room and took the beer out of his hand. Picking up the remote, she pointed it back over her shoulder and turned the TV off.

"Since it's your last night here, I think we've got better things to do than watch the tube, dontcha think?" she asked as she straddled his legs and sat down on his lap.

She leaned in for a kiss, cutting off his response, as his hands reached up under the negligee to her breasts.

"Maybe, this time, before you go, we can try this as a werewolf," she whispered into his ear.

They had actually discussed this, and while Aiden wasn't sure about it, he was at least open to the idea. His varg sure was, but his human side wondered if it was too far, too weird to be OK.

She started grinding into his crotch, and he could feel his blood pound. Ever since he had been turned, he thought his sexual drive was much stronger, but his experiences pre-werewolf had been so limited, he wasn't sure. Stronger or not, it threatened to overcome him.

Claire reached down and unzipped his jeans, a hand grasping him. He gasped and pulled her tighter. He had to get completely out of the jeans, and he pushed her aside. If he'd known they would go at it so soon, he'd have left the Levis off and worn something more accessible. He had to half lift Claire off of him, where she perched, like a porn movie on pause, until he managed to get the jeans off. Then, the play button was punched, and she was back on him as if there was no interruption.

Aiden started to lose it. He wanted to extend the session, to make it longer, but he knew it was early. There was plenty of time for encore performances. There had been almost no foreplay, but he slid into Claire as she sat on his lap.

"You can change now," she said, biting his ear.

His varg roared inside to get out, to take over. He wondered if he should fight it or just let it go. The varg had just about won out when fire lanced through his shoulder, and that snapped him back. He stared incredulously at Claire, her mouth clamped onto his shoulder and she ground down.

Claire? She's into pain? he wondered in shock.

He tried to push her away, but she resisted, clamping down even harder. He tried again with more strength, tearing her off of him.

"What the fuck, Claire?" he asked, his ardor disappearing.

Claire sat back triumphantly, blood streaming down her face. When she reached up and sank her fingernails through his blood and into her cheek, it all clicked into place.

"What the hell did you do, Claire!" he shouted.

"You know what I've done, Aiden. I've joined you!"

Chapter 47

"It's started," Hozan said as Claire started shivering.

When Claire had infected herself, Aiden had gotten on the phone and called the major. Keenan had said he could pull strings, more than a mere major should have been able to pull, so Aiden had demanded that he get Hozan to the States, and that he arrange for both Claire and him to get on TAD[47] orders somewhere together.

The major had not asked questions nor offered recriminations. As soon as Aiden reported back to Lejeune, there were orders waiting for him to go to Ft. Benning. A quick phone call to Claire revealed she had orders there as well. They met up at the Holiday Inn Express in Columbus four days later. Claire enveloped him in a hug, one she didn't seem to want to let go. She was still upbeat and outwardly confident, but Aiden knew she was worried as she realized just what she'd done.

Keenan was in the adjoining room. Aiden hadn't expected him to be there as well, but it would make things easier for them. Two days later, Hozan arrived, his papers all in order.

Hozan was angry, but not as much as Aiden had expected. He had taken Aiden aside, away from the other two, and they'd had a heart-to-heart. Hozan had stressed how dangerous this was, and how they had to keep this from the Council. He'd already scanned the area for others of the Tribe and declared it clear, but there were a hundred ways this could leak out. That could be a death sentence for all four of them, four if Claire managed to survive, that is, something Hozan doubted very much.

The major had obtained a small office space just down the road from the hotel. It had an innocuous front, but in back was a small room. In the room was an athletic tub—the kind athletes soaked in after a game—a bed, IV trees, and some sort of medical

---

[47] TAD: Temporary Additional Duty

contraption. Aiden thought the restraining straps on the bed scared Claire more than anything else.

Aiden only asked Keenan once how he'd arranged for all of this. Keenan said it was better left unsaid, but he did say that all of this was being kept from his boss. Only the four of them knew what was happening.

Aiden and Claire may have been on TAD orders, but they didn't have any real duties. They just killed time, playing cards with each other and the other two, watching TV, and eating what Keenan brought in. Hozan had to be taught poker, but he sucked at it, often quitting in a huff only to come back in 30 minutes to try again. Within a week, he owed the others over $12,000,000 and the country of Iraq north of Mosul.

Hozan and Keenan seemed to form a tight bond as the time progressed. That made Aiden slightly jealous, but his worry about Claire kept that jealousy at bay. When Hozan started to teach Keenan how to shift, despite his assurance that Keenan would not actually be able to achieve it, Claire listened intently. She might be scared, but her warrior's heart would not give up. She was sure she would survive.

After three fruitless days of trying, while Aiden and Claire were eating their KFC, Keenan's body seemed to flow together for a moment before coalescing into a large, silver-streaked varg. Keenan's prosthetic leg clattered to the floor as the varg stood up with two whole legs.

Aiden stopped mid-bite, the chicken leg in his hand, his mouth open. Hozan had thought Keenan would never be able to shift, yet here he had done just that. He remembered how painful the first shift had been, and he could see the panicked look in Keenan's varg eyes.

Immediately, Hozan shifted and put his hands on Keenan's shoulders. He quietly spoke to him, his guttural words too low for Aiden to make out. He remembered how Hozan had calmed him in the Iraqi desert after his first shift. At least Keenan knew what was happening to him. Aiden had been completely in the dark when he shifted without a clue as to what happened.

Claire couldn't take her eyes off of Keenan as Hozan talked him down. It took almost two hours, but finally, Keenan shifted back. He was back to missing a leg, and he seemed dazed as he tried to gather the torn shreds of his shirt around him, but there was a glint of triumph in his eyes. He had done it.

They had both steered clear while Hozan talked Keenan down, but with him back, they went and hugged him. Aiden was just glad that he hadn't killed his friend, for that is what he considered Keenan to be now, but Claire probably hugged him with hope that she could make the journey, too.

"I may not be a werewolf, but I stayed at a Holiday Inn Express last night," Claire said, trying not to laugh.

Both Aiden and Keenan groaned theatrically while Hozan looked confused.

"I bet you've been planning that gem for days," Aiden said, giving his fiancé her own hug.

The fact that the varg Keenan had two whole legs while the human was still missing one was fuel for quite a bit of discussion. They couldn't come up with an explanation that they all could accept.

Keenan tried for the next few days to shift again without success. This didn't concern Hozan. Keenan had done it once, and after he learned the technique, it would become easier.

While Keenan tried to conquer the technique, Claire became more withdrawn. She and Aiden slept together, but he merely held her. There was no sex, no passion. He was there to support her and keep the demons from invading her dreams. When she moaned or muttered in her sleep, he just held her tight until she relaxed.

Ten days after arriving in Columbus, Claire complained of a headache, then sat down as dizziness overcame her. She sat on the end of the bed and started shivering.

Aiden didn't need Hozan to declare the onset of the sickness. Like a father who had rehearsed his wife's delivery of their child, he sprang into motion. He had a small bag packed, and he whipped it up. He sent Hozan to get Keenan from his room, and helped Claire to her feet. By the time he'd helped her out the door, Keenan was there, and the three men got her to the rental car. Two minutes later, they were escorting her into the office and to the back room.

Aiden had to push down the panic that tried to overwhelm him. This was where he could lose his fiancé, and that was something he didn't want to contemplate.

Hozan had already been briefed and rehearsed. He filled the tub with ice and ran the water. Claire was already burning up, so they stripped her and put her in. Aiden sat on the outside and kept her head out of the water. She was only semiconscious by this time, and she was not in control of her body.

It took almost an hour before the bell rang. Keenan stepped out, returning a few moments later with a no-nonsense-looking woman. Aiden didn't know who she was or where Keenan had found her, only that Keenan assured him that she would ask no questions and was reliable. Aiden decided he didn't want to know more, so he left it at that.

"It's too early for the bath," she said professionally, directing the men to take Claire out and put her on the table.

She inserted the IV and started a saline drip.

"In the previous cases, hemodialysis was necessary, you said?" she asked as she examined Claire.

"We believe so," Keenan told her.

"In that case, I'm going to set it up. There could be complications with it, so I intend to be very conservative at first. I can always ramp it up."

Keenan watched as the woman finished her examination. She connected Claire to a bank of monitors, then started the blood line for the hemodialysis machine.

Claire, his strong, vital Claire, looked small and helpless on the table. She was completely unconscious, and whether or not she ever opened her eyes again was up to this middle-aged, overweight woman. Aiden hoped she was more competent than she looked.

Then the wait began. At three hours, Claire started going into convulsions, and the woman injected several drugs into the IV line. That seemed to stop them, and Aiden tried to force his pulse back down.

The woman—Aiden never even asked her name—kept busy, monitoring Claire's vitals. Her temperature climbed to 103, which was lower than Keenan's had been, but still dangerous. The woman adjusted the hemodialysis machine and said she was considering a gastric lavage. Aiden knew that meant something to do with her stomach, but if it would help, he was all for it.

By morning, Claire's temperature had climbed to 105. It was time for the ice bath. They lowered her body into the bath carefully, keeping all the IV and blood lines out of the water. Her body temperature eased back down to 103, but no lower.

She'd had no more convulsions, but the woman mentioned that the drugs that helped control them could be affecting her temperature as well.

Aiden started peppering the woman with questions, so many that Keenan took him aside and told him to go get breakfast. Aiden protested, but the major was pretty adamant, so he walked outside and to a 7-Eleven.

They wanted breakfast? Hostess Pies, jerky, and Cokes would have to do.

He'd calmed down by the time he'd gotten back, and he tried to stay out of the way. He knew the woman was doing the best she could.

That day was hour after glacially moving hour of waiting. Several times they'd put Claire in the ice bath, and once, the woman administered the lavage, something that bothered Aiden to watch more than anything else. Claire had groaned during the procedure, and that tore at him.

For the most part, Claire didn't move. Her body was just a housing for the battle that raged inside of her. Her mind was not there, and all Aiden could do was hope that her mind would somehow find its way back.

Around midnight, Aiden was woken from where he'd been nodding off to a flurry of activity. The woman was barking orders to get Claire into the bath. Aiden saw the body temperature on the readout: 107. As they picked her up, she started spasming. That knocked out two of the IV lines, but they got her in the ice bath while the woman reconnected the lines.

For the first time, the woman showed evidence of panic. She gave orders, ran the hemodialysis again, and administered more meds, but Aiden could see she had lost most of her calm assuredness. That scared the crap out of Aiden.

He grasped Claire's hand as if he could keep her alive by force of will alone.

"We need to get her to a hospital," the woman told Keenan.

"Can they do anything else for her?" he asked.

"No, not really. But I've done about all I can do."

"Can moving her now hurt?"

"Oh, crap! No, we need to keep her here on the hemodialysis. Taking her off could be the end. Sorry, sorry, I'm just afraid we're going to lose her," she said in despair.

"Aiden?" Keenan asked.

"Maybe we should have done that in the beginning, but if we need to keep her hooked up to that blood machine, I think we've got to ride this out," he said, trying to put conviction he didn't feel into his voice.

"You heard the man. It's up to you to pull her through," he told the woman.

It took almost an hour, but finally, the readout hit 106. It was still deadly dangerous, but at least it was lower. Her brain might have been cooked, however, and even if her body survived, Claire would be gone.

Aiden held her hand as the other two dumped more ice in the water. When her temperature slid to 105, the woman told them to take her out. They put her back on the bed, putting ice packs around her. The steady hum of the hemodialysis machine wouldn't let Aiden forget, though, that Claire would be dead by now without modern medical care.

Aiden started crying for the first time since she'd taken sick. He held her hand and put his face next to her shoulder.

"Aiden, let go, you're squeezing my hand too tight," a voice spoke out, worming its way into his consciousness. He opened his eyes, unsure if he'd just dreamed it. Keenan was asleep on a chair, and Hozan was gone. The woman, though, her eyes bloodshot, had turned around from where she was looking at the readouts.

It was morning, and Aiden didn't know how he'd let himself fall asleep.

"Aiden! You're hurting me," Claire said beside him, opening her eyes.

He dropped her hand and jumped up. Keenan woke up with a start, and the woman took two quick steps, peering into Claire's eyes.

"Claire!" was all he could say.

"Am I OK?" she asked. "Did I make it?"

"Yes, young lady. You made it," the woman said, relief in her voice. "You made it!"

Chapter 48

Keenan met him at the entrance, a pass in hand. Aiden was impressed. The building was huge. More than that, he could almost feel the power emanating from it. As Keenan led him down a hall, portraits of civilians hung, almost like an honor guard. People walked purposefully, doing the nation's business.

A three-star general walked by, just like everyone else, without a phalanx of guards preceding him. A three-star!

Aiden had seen the Pentagon on TV before, but actually walking inside was something else, something that could not be conveyed except in person. He'd never thought he would ever be in the Pentagon, but here he was.

Aiden and Claire had stayed in Columbus for five more days. The woman had declared Claire recovered a day after her fever broke and had left accompanied by their heartfelt thanks. Most of the time was spent relaxing and watching TV. They ignored, for the most part, the elephant in the room. Claire had survived the sickness, but was she a werewolf now? On their last night, they had made love again, but it was a gentle, easy act, without real passion but with a depth of feeling.

Three days after returning to Lejeune, he'd received more TAD orders, to Norm's growing frustration. These were to the Pentagon. Norm asked what the orders were about, and Aiden claimed ignorance. It was the truth, though. He could guess, but he didn't know. Norm said he was going to bring it up with the CO, but there wasn't much he could do about it.

Keenan had called him that evening, telling him the orders were from his boss. Keenan would meet him, but other than that, he was out of the loop as to what his colonel knew.

Aiden was nervous, but he craned his neck to take in everything he could. Keenan said they were early, so he took him to a cafeteria where he they had a late breakfast. The place was packed with military and civilians. At the next table, a two-star Marine general was sipping coffee while reading a book. Whatever Aiden had thought the Pentagon was like, this wasn't it. It was like an underground mall, with a book store, a donut shop, even a flower shop!

Keenan looked at his watch and told him they'd better get going. He followed the major back into the passageways, and after ten minutes, with Aiden totally lost, Keenan swiped his card at a door, above which read "Waste Management: Effluent."

Shit management? Aiden wondered.

The door opened into a small group of three offices. Two people were manning desks in the outer office, and a civilian was in a small side office, but Keenan took him to the back office. He rapped at the door, and after hearing an "Enter!" pushed it open.

Aiden followed and entered a small office, but a typical one, with various "I Love Me" plaques and certificates hanging on the walls. The subject of those plaques, Aiden guessed, was the Army colonel standing up behind the lone desk.

Aiden came to attention and stated, "Corporal Aiden Kaas, reporting as ordered, sir!"

"At ease, Marine, at ease. Take a seat," he said, indicating the two chairs against the wall. "And that will be all, Major," he said to Keenan.

Keenan seemed as if he wanted to object, but he said nothing and left the office.

"Colonel Jack Tarniton, son. Good to finally meet you," he said, coming from around the desk, hand out to be shaken.

Aiden took the proffered hand, and as the colonel sat down on the front edge of his desk, he took the seat, sitting on the edge in the "sitting position of attention."

"Relax, son, you're not in any trouble. I'm here to help you."

"Sir?"

"Son, Aiden—can I call you Aiden?" he said, then proceeding before Aiden could respond. "It has come to our attention, to my attention, that you have been the target of foreign aggression."

What?

"The assault on your mother, and more recently, in Hawaii, were the acts of a foreign interest."

"Sir? You know about all of that? Who did that?" he asked excitedly.

"As to who, we are not quite sure. I think the Russians, myself. And we didn't know the reason for this. I mean, no disrespect intended, but why target a Marine corporal? I sent Major Ward to watch over you, to protect you while we investigated it. And at last we found out."

Found out what? What do you know?

"We know what you are. As hard as it is to believe, you are a werewolf," the colonel said with a sense of satisfaction.

"Sir? I mean, that's crazy!"

"Ah, keeping it close to the vest. Smart move, young man, considering. But you see, Aiden—I asked if I could call you that, right? You see, we intercepted a transmission a couple of weeks back, when you were in Hawaii. It was encrypted, and we only managed to crack the encryption a couple of days ago. Do you want to see what we saw?"

With his heart pounding, he said "Yes, sir."

The colonel picked up a laptop, a thumb drive sticking out of a USB port. He clicked on the mousepad a few times, then turned the laptop around so Aiden could see it.

The video was dark, and things were hard to make out. The tinny words, though, brought it into focus:

"Hey, haole. How 'bout you give us your wallet, yeah?"

The video was bouncing around, but he could clearly see himself, trying to get in front of Claire. There was no question about that.

"Look, we don't want any trouble," his voice sounded.

The scene played out, the give and take, until the leader said, "Oh, you like beef? I think it's time to kick your man's okole. You ready to give um, little man?"

The next few scenes were rushed as the leader charged Aiden, knocking him to the ground. The camera, which had to have been on the leader, was not the best, and there were flashes of fists and Aiden's face. The scene heaved, and Aiden was back in focus. Suddenly, the ground flashed up.

That's my Claire punching the shit out of him, he thought with pride.

Then there was Claire's scream, followed by a roar, a roar that Aiden knew was him. The camera jerked as the man tried to get to his feet, and there were flashes that Aiden knew were of him killing the other two men. It wasn't clear, however, and Aiden still hoped he could explain it away. But when Aiden marched up to the man in all his varg power, there was no doubt about it. He was a werewolf

"Who sent you?" his guttural words reached out from the laptop.

"Someone bigger than you," the man said. "And now I know why."

The camera was aimed at Aiden's chest as he squeezed the life out of the man. The scene was vivid and clear. When he dropped the man, the camera was mercifully turned towards the dirt. But there was one more piece of damning evidence.

It was his, "Claire, it's me. Aiden!"

"There's more there," the colonel said, but it's of you and your girlfriend putting the bodies in the trunk, of taking them out and dumping them in the surf. But as you can see, we know now why they are after you. They cannot allow the United States to have a werewolf in its armed forces. Imagine what that would mean!"

"Am I in trouble, sir?"

"Trouble? Good God, no. Why would you be in trouble?"

"I killed those three men," he said.

"You killed three enemy agents, son. You were doing your duty to keep America safe. I would have been disappointed in you if you hadn't killed those scum. You would be no use to me if you'd turned coward."

No use to him? What is he getting at?

"Sir, what do you mean?" he asked.

"Our enemies want to eliminate you as a threat. Why? Because they know you can be of great service to your country. They can't allow that to happen. But the cowards that they are, they tried and get to you through your mother, through your girlfriend."

"So what do you want me to do, sir?" Aiden asked.

"Fight the bastards! Don't let them threaten you! Don't let them threaten your loved ones. Don't let them threaten your country for God's sake!"

If they were going to threaten his family, then Aiden had to do something. But just who were "they?" What the colonel was saying made sense. If the colonel wanted, he could just lock him up and throw away the key. He seemed earnest enough, though, wanting his cooperation, not trying to force it.

Aiden had sworn an oath as a Marine to "support and defend the Constitution of the United States," and to "obey the orders of those officers appointed over him." Wasn't it his duty to do just that?

He knew that Hozan would not agree to the direction the colonel was going. The Tribe did not get involved in the affairs of men. But hadn't Hozan himself fought in the Peshmerga Army? What was that if not getting involved?

"Are you a patriot?" the colonel asked.

"Of course I am, sir," Aiden burst out saying without even thinking about the answer.

He was a Marine, and all Marines loved their country.

"OK, then. That should be it. If you are a patriot, you will do your duty. And I shouldn't have to add, I will be doing everything to protect your mother and girlfriend. You won't have to worry about that.

"I do need one thing first. I showed you the transmission we intercepted. But I need to ask you, one military man to another, are you a werewolf?"

Aiden hesitated. It had been drilled into him that he needed to keep that secret. But the man had a recording, and he was a full-bird colonel. He couldn't lie to him.

"Yes, sir."

The colonel seemed to relax, and then he said, "I believe you, but for my own sake, I want to see it before I commit myself to your cause, to put my resources to work for you. Can you change yourself for me?"

Again Aiden hesitated. He wasn't sure why, though. He'd just admitted it. He made up his mind.

"I need to take off my uniform," he said.

He stood up, then slowly stripped down to his boxers. It was pretty surreal, here in the Pentagon, down to his boxers in front of a bird colonel. The colonel was looking at him expectantly, so without any more hesitation, he turned his mental switch and shifted.

The colonel took an involuntary step back as he looked up at the varg standing before him.

"Holy shit, it's true," he said, astonished. "I mean, I knew it was, but seeing you—holy shit!"

Epilogue

The colonel looked through the one-way mirror at the sleeping Kaas. He was elated, no question about it. He'd known Kaas was a werewolf, but when the kid transformed himself, right in the office, he'd about shit himself. He, Colonel Jack Tarniton, three times passed over for his star, had uncovered the ultimate soldier. And now that soldier belonged to him, not only willing, but anxious to do his bidding.

After Kaas had shifted back, he'd gotten the kid to sign a non-disclosure document. He'd pulled it off the Internet, added some heavy-sounding sentences, and printed it up. It wasn't worth squat, but he was sure Kaas didn't know that and would have been impressed by its importance. The colonel wanted secrecy, and the document, along with some BS he'd thrown at him, should do the trick.

The kid was susceptible to BS, that was for sure. He'd bought the Russian angle hook, line, and sinker. He wondered if Kaas even noticed when he'd shifted the conversation from what Kaas could do for him to what he could do to help Kaas. He had remembered that trick from a business class he'd taken in school. If he could get a person to assume ownership of an idea or concept, he could get a more dedicated worker, or in this case, a soldier.

He'd escorted Kaas out of the office, much to the consternation of that prick, Ward. The major was up to something, that was for certain. He'd played out some little game the week before, going down to Ft. Benning, and the colonel had not gotten to the bottom of it yet, but he would. If it weren't for the fact that the major was now probably a werewolf, too, the guy would be out of the Army on his one-legged ass.

The major didn't know about the holding rooms in the depths of the Pentagon. The colonel had escorted Aiden to one of them, telling him they needed to go through some tests before they could decide what they could do to help him. The colonel actually had conducted some tests, such as strength and mobility. The werewolf Kaas was very, very strong. His dexterity was a disappointment, though, and the colonel realized he might have to modify some of the ideas he'd had for weapons for a werewolf task force. He looked forward to taking Kaas out for field trials.

Telling Kaas it was later than it really was, he suggested that he gets some rest. He assured him that he would leave the Pentagon in the morning, that they only had a few more things to do.

Kaas agreed, and after pacing the room for 30 minutes, laid down in bed and closed his eyes. The colonel watched him until the steady rise and fall of Kaas chest indicated that he was asleep.

There were a few hidden capabilities of these rooms that were not immediately obvious, but were very useful. What went on in these rooms was highly classified, but the colonel's imagination ran wild as he wondered what had gone on in them over the last 70 years. It buggered the imagination.

He checked on Kaas one more time, then flipped a switch. From a vent at the top of the room, an odorless gas descended to envelope the kid. Kaas gave a grunt, but then went quiet. The colonel waited for ten minutes, watching for any sign of movement. He had no idea how a werewolf would react to the gas, but he put enough in there to knock out an elephant.

He slipped on an oxygen mask and carefully opened the door into the room. Kaas didn't stir. His nerves were jumping as he walked up to the sleeping form.

This is it! he thought.

Taking the syringe he'd prepared, he pressed the needle into Kaas arm and pulled back. Nothing showed up. He repositioned the needle, trying to hit the kid's artery. This was harder than he'd thought it would be, especially while trying to see out of the mask. He tried twice more before he was rewarded with the bright scarlet blood filling the tube.

Kaas gave another grunt and twitched, which almost caused the colonel to jerk back and drop his precious blood. He had enough, he hoped. He didn't want to try and find the artery again.

The colonel hurried out of the room and back to the control room. He turned off the gas and turned on the exhaust fan. He wasn't sure if he saw any difference in Kaas' sleep, but it really didn't matter anymore.

He took off his shirt and bared his arm. The colonel barely hesitated before he plunged the needle into his arm and pushed the plunger home. He'd already checked blood types, and both Kaas and he were O+. But Ward was B+, and he was fine, so he wasn't sure blood type mattered. What mattered was what made a werewolf a werewolf. And now that was inside of him. He was going to be one!

Let some asshole try and shoulder him out of the way now! As the commanding officer of a werewolf legion, he would hold all the cards.

World, stand the fuck by! Colonel Jack Tarniton is about to make his mark!

Thank you for reading Book 2 of Werewolf of Marines. I hope you enjoyed it, and I would welcome any feedback on the book's page on Amazon.

The Return of the Marines Trilogy
The Few
The Proud
The Marines

The Al Anbar Chronicles: First Marine Expeditionary Force--Iraq
Prisoner of Fallujah
Combat Corpsman
Sniper

The United Federation Marine Corps
Recruit
Sergeant
Lieutenant
Major (Coming Soon)

Rebel

Werewolf of Marines
Semper Lycanus
Patria Lycanus

To The Shores of Tripoli

Wererat

Darwin's Quest: The Search for the Ultimate Survivor

Venus: A Paleolithic Short Story

Non-Fiction

Exercise for a Longer Life

Author Website

Jonathan P. Brazee

Made in the USA
San Bernardino, CA
08 April 2015